"First," he said, "I decide the place."

"And then?" she asked, clearly skeptical.

"Then, if we agree on the first step, we move on to the next."

She seemed surprised that he had agreed to consider her plan. He would deal with the official side of this mess as soon as Grace and Liam were someplace safe, and he knew just the place.

"Okay. Where do you have in mind?"

"I have a place kind of off-the-grid. It's isolated and difficult to find."

She nodded. "Sounds good. I have a bag with some extra cash and new IDs. Everything we need to..."

As if she'd realized that it sounded exactly like she planned to disappear, her voice trailed off.

"I get it." He shrugged. "You're prepared to run if necessary. You will gladly give up everything to keep him safe."

She squeezed her eyes shut for a moment before meeting his gaze once more. "I would. Including my life."

Author Note

With all the books I write, I love finding the perfect homes for my characters. Deciding on their occupations is equally important to me. The Lookout Inn is based on a real inn on Lookout Mountain. I won't tell you the name but I'll bet you can find it. Mockingbird Lane is actually on the Georgia side of the mountain but I loved it so I decided to do a little adjusting. The cabin I gave Rob Vaughn is also a real place on the Tennessee River. It's gorgeous! Really, I just love charming communities and historic homes. It's an absolute pleasure for me to get to live in those places vicariously through my characters and stories. I hope you enjoy reading this story as much as I enjoyed writing it! Cheers!

A PLACE TO HIDE

USA TODAY Bestselling Author
DEBRA WEBB

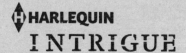

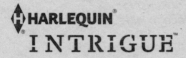

Recycling programs for this product may not exist in your area.

ISBN-13: 978-1-335-59144-9

A Place to Hide

Harlequin Enterprises ULC
22 Adelaide St. West, 41st Floor
Toronto, Ontario M5H 4E3, Canada
www.Harlequin.com

Printed in U.S.A.

Debra Webb is the award-winning *USA TODAY* bestselling author of more than one hundred novels, including those in reader-favorite series Faces of Evil, the Colby Agency and Shades of Death. With more than four million books sold in numerous languages and countries, Debra has a love of storytelling that goes back to her childhood on a farm in Alabama. Visit Debra at debrawebb.com.

Books by Debra Webb

Harlequin Intrigue

Lookout Mountain Mysteries

Disappearance in Dread Hollow
Murder at Sunset Rock
A Place to Hide

A Winchester, Tennessee Thriller

In Self Defense
The Dark Woods
The Stranger Next Door
The Safest Lies
Witness Protection Widow
Before He Vanished
The Bone Room

Colby Agency: Sexi-ER

Finding the Edge
Sin and Bone
Body of Evidence

Faces of Evil

Dark Whispers
Still Waters

Visit the Author Profile page at Harlequin.com.

CAST OF CHARACTERS

Grace Myers—She's finally found peace and happiness, but will her past destroy all that she's worked so hard to build for herself and her son, Liam?

Robert "Rob" Vaughn—As the sheriff's deputy in charge, it's his job to keep the citizens of Lookout Mountain safe, but can he do that when the bodies start piling up?

Liam—He's a brave boy and he just wants his mommy to be happy.

Cara Gunther—She is Grace's right hand. Liam adores her. But she knows things that Grace can't remember...does that make her friend or foe?

Diane Franks—Chef extraordinaire. Grace trusts Diane completely, but will that trust be her downfall?

Adam Locke—A monster...a serial killer. Grace's ex-husband is back and he intends to have his son... and his vengeance.

Detective Lance Gibbons—The San Francisco detective who tried to bring Adam Locke down. Has he come to finish the job he started or to make Grace pay?

Joe Pierce—A reporter from Los Angeles who just happens to show up when the body count starts.

Chapter One

The Lookout Inn
Mockingbird Lane
Lookout Mountain, Tennessee
Sunday, February 18, 5:00 p.m.

The last guest had checked out and the inn was quiet.

Grace Myers wandered through the lobby. Despite having every reason not to ever smile again, she smiled. She loved this place. She crossed to the French doors that led onto the terrace. Never in a million years had she expected to be this happy again. Not ever.

She walked out into the crisp winter air and inhaled deeply.

But she was okay now. Really okay.

How long had it been since she'd really smiled? Smiled and felt it all the way to her bones?

Two years and ten months. One thousand thirty-two days.

Every single one of those days had been painful and terrifying, but the intensity had begun to lessen since Christmas. A part of her had started to get comfortable. Now, *this* felt like home. Her life felt like her own.

Another deep breath and she hugged herself against the cold. She hadn't bothered with a jacket. Grace had wanted to feel the cold. To stand out here staring at that amazing view of the valley below, feeling the icy air penetrating her sweatshirt and jeans. It was a welcome reminder that she was alive. More important, her precious little boy was alive. And they were free of the threat that had almost killed them both. They had not only survived—they had thrived.

Grace shivered at those old painful memories before slamming a mental door, banishing them to a rarely visited place. She gazed out over the views from her mountaintop perch one last time before going back inside. Liam would be waking up from his nap soon. He would be frightened if he woke up alone. Though his fear was natural at his age, she couldn't say as much for her own. She wasn't sure how long it would take for her to overcome the panic of being more than a few steps away from him.

She closed and secured the door. Then she moved around the lobby and ensured the others were as well. Usually she didn't lock the main entrance until midnight, but her guests had all checked out and she wasn't expecting anyone else until tomorrow. There was the rare occasion when an unexpected guest arrived, but he or she could press the doorbell.

An evening of solitude with her favorite little man would be a nice change of pace. The inn had been for the most part solidly booked through the Christmas and

New Year season, and busy all the way to Valentine's Day. At least ten of the twenty guest rooms had been occupied all that time until today. It was a great winter season, and she was genuinely grateful. Just maybe this was a sign of things to come.

Good things.

Honestly, it was still difficult to grasp the idea that this place was hers. She stalled, gazed around the large space that served as the lobby. Hundred-and-fifty-year-old shiplap walls soared some thirty feet to a beamed and vaulted ceiling that still took her breath away. The vintage chandeliers and numerous windows and sets of French doors filled the space with light. The stone on the floor was the same stone that covered the exterior facade and climbed the better part of the far wall in the lobby where a massive fireplace added a homey feeling. It was more beautiful than any home or business she could ever have hoped to own.

When she'd bought it, the inn had been empty for years. The former owners had retired to Florida with the idea of perhaps leasing out the property. The couple hadn't been able to adjust to the idea of someone else running the inn. Eventually they'd had no choice but to sell in order to prevent the property from falling into disrepair. A vacant home—or inn—lost its soul when empty of people and slowly fell apart. Grace had taken one look at the place and known this was the dream she wanted for herself and her son. She and Liam had gone to Florida and spoken to the elderly owners. Forty-eight hours later, the property was theirs. As triumphant as she had felt at that moment, that had only been the beginning.

Months and months of hard work were required to bring the inn back to life—to infuse vibrancy into it once more. Lucky for Grace the bones had all been there; she'd only needed to tweak the mechanics like the electrical and the heating and cooling systems and then spruce up the rest cosmetically. Finding the perfect furnishings for their private quarters had been the most difficult. The previous owners had taken their personal furnishings with them to Florida. Months of frequenting vintage shops and perusing online dealers had paid off. Luckily the French drapes tailor-made for the many large windows had only required cleaning. The same went for the numerous Persian rugs. The furnishings in the common areas and the guest rooms had been perfect and only in need of polishing.

It had all come together beautifully. The ridiculously happy smile slid across her face once more. She wasn't sure she would ever stop smiling again. A good thing, she decided.

Before returning to the registration desk to tidy up, she placed a couple more logs on the fire. Sparks flared and a hint of oaky smoke stirred. Until she'd started this new life, she hadn't realized there was such a variety of scents when it came to firewood. For the most part she bought hickory. The scent was classic, very traditional. But cherry was her favorite by far. She used the cherry for special occasions, like Christmas.

She dusted her hands together and moved on to the registration desk, where she locked the drawers and ensured all was as it should be. A few taps and the computer system went dark and silent. From there she moved through the dining room. The tables had been cleared and prepped for the next meal, which wouldn't be until lunch tomorrow, when her guests were due.

She paused, rested her hands on the back of a chair. More lovely sets of French doors in the dining room provided access to the terrace that flanked both sides of the structure where it overlooked the valley below. The view was simply incredible. She wandered there, gazed out for a few moments before testing the locks. Once those doors were checked she continued to the large kitchen. Her chest squeezed the tiniest bit. How she loved this kitchen. Vintage in every way save the appliances.

The back-door lock was secure. This was a nightly ritual for her. A desperate need time would never assuage. Though she had an alarm system, it wasn't the best. Later she hoped to upgrade, but that was one expense that would have to wait.

With all as it should be, she sneaked quietly into their private suite. Liam slept like a precious little lamb. Generally he was up well before now, but his usual one o'clock nap hadn't happened until past three. He lay in the middle of the big bed. He had his own small room right next to hers, but she hadn't been able to move him there just yet. She wanted him with her at night. Some would scold her for the decision, but they had not lived through what she had survived.

Their suite included a small parlor and a kitchenette as well as a nice-sized bathroom. It really was all quite small compared to the size of the inn, but it was everything they needed and she loved it. It felt cozy and comfortable. Of the twenty guest quarters, there were ten rooms with en suites upstairs as well as ten more small cottages that had been added to the property fifty or so years ago. The additions formed a semicircle on either side of the rear gardens. Each cottage had an enviable view of the valley below.

Grace climbed carefully onto the bed with her child. She had never been one to take afternoon naps, but she had been working really hard for months and it was starting to catch up with her. She needed a break. A little getaway.

She almost laughed at the idea. Maybe by summer's end, late August perhaps, she would be able to afford a short time away. Certainly, that would be low season. Maybe she would take Liam to his favorite theme park. Every time he saw a commercial about the place, he jumped up and down and shouted in delight.

His blond hair was just a tad curly and brushed his shoulders. There were moments when she chastised herself for not giving him his first haircut yet. Whenever they dropped in at any of the local shops, most people they encountered thought he was a little girl, but frankly, she was glad. Being seen with a little girl was less likely to put her on anyone's radar since the one person who—if given the chance—might ever look for her would be looking for a woman with a little boy. She swallowed hard against the thought. Her little boy's eyes were closed, but she knew them by heart. He had the most vivid blue eyes. Like the sky on a frosty morning.

Grace closed her eyes and thought of the last time she had seen her father and how amazed he had been by his grandson. William Reinhart had adored his namesake. Their time together had been far too short. The memory ached deep in her chest.

Her father's sudden death was her fault. She shouldn't have taken her problems to his door, but she'd had no place else to go. Even now—if he were alive and despite what had happened—her father would insist that she had made the right decision. Of course he would. But she should have taken care of herself   after all, it was her fault she'd ended up in trouble. Ultimately, her choices had been limited because it hadn't been just about her. She'd had to protect Liam, and to do that, she had needed help. Desperation had dictated her decisions.

Maybe her father wouldn't have suffered that massive heart attack if she and Liam had run in a different direction. Didn't that make his death her fault?

Before her mind could come up with an acceptable rebuttal, sleep dragged her into its tumultuous depths.

HE SCREAMED HER NAME.

The sound echoed through her, sending terror through her veins. The knowledge that she was dead if he caught her shuddered through her very soul.

You're dreaming. Wake up!

But she couldn't. She was in too deep.

She had to run faster. But it was so cold… The snow was deep and dragging at her feet; the woods were dense and foreboding. She was lost in the darkness. It was only that damned snow catching the light of the moon that prevented her from running headlong into a tree or over a cliff.

Keep going.

Don't stop.

The bare trees loomed over her like shadowy creatures backlit by that big moon. A hint of familiarity had hope fizzing through her. Was she almost to the highway? A new burst of adrenaline fired in her blood. Maybe just a little farther now. If she reached the main highway, someone might come along and stop for her. She could get to help then.

All she had to do was make it to the highway.

Another pain deep in her belly forced her to a stop, made her cry out.

The baby was coming.

Dear God, she had to keep going…had to hurry. Her feet began to move again. She stumbled forward. Panted for breath.

Please, please let her get out of these woods and to help before the baby was born. She blinked back the burn of tears and rushed forward a little faster, staggering and lurching. She was so, so cold now. Her feet felt like leaden weights, her legs stiff and unresponsive.

Don't stop.

She pushed onward. Almost there.

The sound of a car's engine humming along in the distance gave her hope, sparked her determination not to give up. She could do this! She could make it. All she had to do was keep going.

Grace broke through the tree line. The inky black highway cut a winding path for miles through the trees, snow and ice lining the shoulders and ditches on both sides. She scrambled down and then up from the ditch and staggered onto the slick pavement.

Air sawed in and out of her lungs as she gasped for breath. Had the car passed this point already?

Please, please let another one come along.

She winced as she tightened her fingers into fists, the bones feeling as if they were breaking, her skin numb from the cold. There had been no time for gloves, no time for anything but to run.

He'd shown up unexpectedly, and she'd had no other choice except to get out of there. She'd had to abandon everything. Every. Single. Thing.

The only thing that really mattered was still inside her…the *baby*.

She prayed he wouldn't find her before another car came along.

The distant sound of something—a vehicle, she hoped—brushed against her senses.

She started in that direction, barely maintaining her balance on the slippery asphalt.

The sound came closer and closer. Finally, she saw the headlights. Grace braced herself to keep her balance and started to wave her arms.

"Help me," she cried out, her voice weak and not nearly loud enough. "Help!"

The gush of warmth that flowed down her legs warned her that her water had broken. She grabbed at herself. "Oh, God."

The car started to slow. She waved one arm, held her belly with the other. "Please! Please!"

The car stopped and she reached for the door handle, her fingers so cold she couldn't make them work. The door suddenly popped open as if the driver had understood and leaned over and opened it.

"Thank you." She pulled the door open wider and collapsed into the seat. "My baby is coming." She turned to the driver. "I need—"

It was him.

The man who had the same blond hair and blue eyes as her son smiled at her. And she knew her fate.

She was dead.

GRACE BOLTED UPRIGHT, her eyes searching the darkness.

A dream. It had only been a dream.

She pressed a hand to her chest and forced her breathing to slow. She reached her free hand to the lamp and turned on the light. What time was it? Six p.m. flashed on the digital clock. She'd slept for well over an hour.

"Liam." He should be awake by now.

She reached for her son, but beside her the bed was empty…and cold.

Fear slammed into her chest. She jumped from the bed and looked around the room. "Liam!"

She never went to sleep like that. And even if she did, any move or sound he made generally woke her.

She searched the room. Hurried to the parlor. No Liam.

He wasn't anywhere in their private space.

Her gaze landed on the door. It was ajar. As she rushed across the room and through that door, she reminded herself that her little boy, who was not yet three, could not unlock the entry doors. He would be somewhere in the house. The realization should have calmed her but it did not.

"Liam!" She moved from room to room, the kitchen, the dining room, calling his name.

Then she spotted him.

He stood in the lobby staring out the window nearest the fireplace. She rushed to him.

"Liam." She dropped to her knees and turned him toward her, visually examining him from head to toe. "Are you all right?"

He nodded his curly blond head. "I watching the man in the snow."

Grace frowned and stared out the window. It had snowed. Not so much really, just a thin coat of white. She shuddered. She'd been dreaming about running through the snow. The memory had left a bitter taste in her mouth and a cold stone in her gut.

She scanned the landscape as best she could with nothing but the moonlight and a few exterior lights that weren't nearly bright enough, she decided. "I don't see anyone."

"Gone. Gone," her little boy said with a giggle.

Had he been dreaming and only imagined a figure in the darkness?

Grace's gaze searched the snow once more…and her heart stalled.

There, in the newly fallen blanket of snow where the cobblestones led to the front entrance, were tracks. Too large to be any sort of animal. Too well formed to be anything other than boots or shoes.

Liam was right. Someone had been here.

She rose to her feet and surveyed the yard and the steps. She could see where the prints seemed to come from the thick line of shrubbery and crossed the yard, then came up the steps to disappear since there was no snow on the covered porch.

"Me want it."

Grace shook herself. She knelt back down to her little boy. "I'm sorry, sweetie. What did you say?"

"Me want it." Liam pointed to the window.

Grace followed his chubby finger to the porch, but there was nothing there. "Mommy doesn't see anything."

"Down there!" he urged.

She leaned closer to the glass and stared at the stone floor of the porch. The small silver object glinted in the light from the window and had her heart pitching to a near stop.

A heart-shaped locket on a chain.

She didn't have to touch it or even to see it more clearly to know it would be vintage and blood would be smeared on the chain and maybe inside the locket.

Grace grabbed Liam and ran back to their private

space. She closed the door, sat Liam on the floor and engaged the security bar she had ordered just for a moment like this. She backed away, tugging Liam with her.

She had to call the police.

Entering the digits, she collapsed on the floor and pulled Liam into her lap. When the dispatcher answered, she said, "We've had an intruder on the property at the Lookout Inn on Mockingbird Lane. Can you please send someone?"

She had wanted to sound calm but her voice had been thin and hollow. Liam stared at her, his face ready to pucker into tears. He was frightened. She should have been more careful not to upset him.

When she'd answered all the dispatcher's questions and had the promise that a cruiser was en route, Grace ended the call. She held tightly on to the cell phone while hugging Liam to her chest.

"What's wrong, Mommy?"

"Everything's okay, buddy." She rocked back and forth as much for her own benefit as for her child's.

She told herself it couldn't have been him. He was in police custody awaiting trial.

He would never be free again after what he'd done. There was no reason for her to be afraid…none.

But what if she was wrong? She had been wrong before.

A MERE FIFTEEN minutes later, the police had arrived and begun the search of the property outside the inn. Before the deputies had started roving the landscape, she, with Liam on her hip, had slipped onto the porch and picked up the locket. She'd done so using a plastic sandwich baggie so as not to touch it. She'd opened it using the bag to protect her fingers. A bloodstained picture of her had been trimmed down to fit inside. She'd closed it instantly. Then she'd taken it to the kitchen and hidden it under the sink. She'd distracted Liam with two chocolate coins. The child loved the gold-wrapped goodies—pirate booty, he would say. The kind in his favorite animated movie. She hated using sweets to bribe him, but sometimes there was just no other option.

The entire search by the police took an hour since the deputies felt it best to have a look around inside as well. Grace didn't have a problem with that. She wanted to be certain whoever had been out there was gone. She told herself again that it couldn't be him.

Impossible.

If she really believed this, why was she hiding the locket from the deputies?

Grace dismissed the thought. It had to be a coincidence. Some local yahoo who was reliving Halloween. Or a true crime fanatic who liked playing games. Her nightmare had dominated the headlines and online news feeds for months. The bastard who'd created that nightmare had quickly gained a bizarre cult following. The first Halloween after she escaped him, some manufacturer had even created and sold a mask of his face. How sick was that?

She shivered. This had to be some serial killer buff playing games. Couldn't be anything else.

But was her certainty only wishful thinking?

Finally, one of the deputies—Scott Reynolds—came into the main parlor to announce they were finished.

"Beyond the tracks, we didn't find anything," he explained. "You said your son saw someone."

Grace looked over at her child, playing with a puzzle at the coffee table that sat between two sofas. "I woke up and he'd climbed out of the bed. I found him in the lobby staring out a window. He said he'd been watching a man in the snow. That's when I noticed the tracks."

Reynolds glanced at Liam. "He said a man."

Grace nodded. "The tracks came up the steps, so I'm guessing the intruder came onto the porch and maybe all the way to the window where Liam was watching." Her stomach tied into a thousand screaming knots at the idea.

Reynolds lowered into a chair. He glanced at his notepad. "Ma'am, I'm not meaning to pry, but I have to ask—where is his father?" He nodded toward Liam.

Folks in the area knew Grace was a single mother. She'd been here almost two years. She and Liam had fit fairly well into the community, though she had been careful not to get too close to anyone. Keeping a certain distance was essential. Getting close to anyone required a willingness to share history, to be open. She couldn't do that. At least, not yet.

"He—" she cleared her throat and lowered her voice "—passed away before we moved here."

Reynolds nodded. "Sorry to hear that." He made a note on his pad. "If you don't mind, I'd like to ask Liam a few questions to see if he remembers anything about the man."

Worry that Liam would mention the object the man left on the porch tore at her. "We could try. He's more likely to respond to me." Her child was on the shy side when it came to talking to anyone he hadn't met before.

Reynolds nodded his understanding. "Just ask him general description questions. Big? Small? Dark? Light?"

Grace nodded. "Okay."

The deputy prepared to jot down any responses onto his notepad.

"Liam." He looked up and Grace motioned for him to come to her. "Deputy Reynolds and I have some questions about the man."

Liam eyed Reynolds speculatively, then walked over to climb into his mother's lap.

"'Kay." His fingers went to his mouth. He did that when he was nervous.

"Was the man you saw big?" She nodded to Reynolds. "Tall like the deputy or shorter like Mommy?"

Liam pointed to Reynolds with his free hand.

"So tall like Deputy Reynolds?"

Liam nodded.

"Did you see his hair?"

Liam moved his head side to side. "Hat." He patted the top of his head.

Reynolds nodded. "Did he wear a hat like mine?"

He picked up the baseball-style cap he'd placed on his knee when he sat down.

Liam scooted out of his mother's lap and ran toward their private quarters.

Reynolds made a face. "You think I scared him off?"

Grace stood. "Give me a moment and I'll see if he will come back."

As if her words had summoned him, Liam ran back into the room. He held one of his favorite beanies.

"Like dis." He held up the beanie.

Reynolds grinned. "All right. Good job, little man." He jotted down the information. "What about his eyes?" He looked to Liam once more. "Did you see what color his eyes were?"

Liam had warmed up to the deputy now. He touched his own eyes. "Mine."

Grace's heart dropped to her feet. "He had blue eyes?"

Liam nodded. "Mine."

Grace lowered back into her chair for fear her knees would buckle any second.

"Great job!" Reynolds praised the boy. "Was he wearing blue jeans like your mom?"

Liam shook his head. "Like Batman."

Grace found her voice again. "So black. All over like Batman? Pants and shirt?"

Liam nodded.

"And gloves too?" Grace lifted her hand.

Once more Liam nodded.

"Thank you, Liam," the deputy said. "You've been very helpful." He closed his notepad and stood. "Ms. Myers, I'll let you know if we figure anything out, although I have to say we don't have much to go on. We did take photos of the boot prints and we are questioning neighbors. But considering the gloves, we're not likely to find prints."

"I understand." She stood. "I just appreciate you coming."

When the deputies were gone, she made Liam a sandwich, poured him a glass of milk and settled him in front of the television. She went to the main kitchen and retrieved the plastic bag from beneath the sink.

She opened it and peered inside. Her gut clenched.

It was the same type of locket the bastard had left behind with his murder victims. Blood smears and all. But why was her picture inside?

Because he wanted her to be his next victim.

With a chill dancing down her spine, she wadded the bag around the damned thing, her eyes closing in defeat.

How could this be? He couldn't know where she was. But he must. It was the only way to explain this. She wanted to believe that, worst-case scenario, he had located them somehow and sent some paid thug or crazed fan to drop off the locket. But Liam said the man had his eyes. Would he have specifically sought out the help of a man with pale blue eyes? Or had the eyes been colored contacts?

Maybe. The bastard was evil to the core.

He would do anything to terrify her.

Would he send the creep back for another visit? Or worse, to hurt them?

She steadied herself. First, she had to make sure he was still in custody. He had to be. He'd been charged with murder and he'd tried to kill her. Bail had been denied.

If Adam Locke, the infamous Sweetheart Killer, was out, wouldn't she have heard?

Of course not. She'd given no one her new address or her new name. How could anyone contact her? Her goal had been to disappear.

Since she hadn't bothered to see what was happening with his trial in a long while, she had no idea if it had even begun. Just hearing his name made her feel ill. Seeing photos of him was more than she could bear.

But now she had no choice.

She had spent the past two years building Liam a safe home here on Lookout Mountain. She had ensured that no one from their old life knew where they were, and no one here knew their true identities.

Was her decision two years ago to disappear—avoiding witness protection or any other support—a mistake? Was keeping her identity here a secret—especially now in light of what had just happened—yet another misstep?

No. She had made the right choices. The only way to protect Liam was for no one anywhere to know their location. As for the locket, until she could be certain this was not some prankster, she wasn't sharing that detail with anyone.

But then…if Adam had found them and had sent this person, how would she ever keep Liam safe?

Chapter Two

Hamilton County Sheriff's Substation
Lookout Mountain
Monday, February 19, 9:25 a.m.

Robert Vaughn shuffled through the messages on his desk. How had he received so many calls on a Sunday evening? The last time he'd gotten that many calls in one stretch was on his birthday. The Mountain was generally far too quiet for this much excitement.

Didn't matter. He couldn't have answered any of them while transporting a violent criminal. His cell phone had stayed in the console of the SUV he'd been driving—on silent. He'd dropped the prisoner off in Knoxville and headed back, not rolling into his own driveway until four this morning.

The two hours' sleep he'd gotten before being called to an accident at seven this morning was not enough sleep to have his brain operating on full power, but he hadn't wanted to take the day off.

More coffee. He needed another shot of caffeine if he was going to survive the morning.

Leaving his closet-sized office, he headed for the break room, which was really just a niche in the corridor leading to the lobby. He refilled his mug and wandered into the small lobby. There was a bench and a coatrack but no room for much else. Beyond this space was another, slightly larger office that was shared by the four other deputies assigned to this substation. Rob was the deputy in charge. The only other space was a storeroom, which served as a multipurpose area. The tight squeeze was all temporary while the new substation for the community was being built. Just more growing pains. The Mountain was expanding.

Rob liked the assignment even with the expansion. He'd been on the mountain for a year, and it still surprised him that he felt completely satisfied here. He'd always considered himself a city boy. So when the opportunity to serve as the deputy in charge of a small community substation had come up, he'd expected to turn it down. But then he'd shocked himself by saying yes.

So maybe it hadn't been such a shock considering he'd been single for nearly a year and he'd needed change. Having the woman he'd expected to marry take off with a deputy from a neighboring community had proved just a little unsettling. Truth was, he'd felt as if they were drifting apart months before she actually split. Still, his ego had been bruised and he'd moped around for a while. The move had come at a good time.

No regrets to this point. He'd even sold his condo in Chattanooga and rented a small studio apartment only a couple of miles from the substation. When he needed total solitude, he spent a few days at his cabin in the woods, perched on the Tennessee River. He'd changed from a sports car to an SUV. Made sense, anyway. The old truck he'd inherited from his father that stayed at the cabin on the river was not four-wheel drive, and sometimes he needed the extra muscle to get up the mountain.

He spent his time in jeans and muck boots when not on duty. He chuckled and shook his head. Maybe there was something about approaching forty that had changed him. Not that thirty-seven was over the hill, but he damned sure wasn't getting any younger. If he was totally honest with himself, starting a family was something he'd hoped to do by now, and that hadn't worked out either.

Banishing that line of thinking, he walked back to his office. Those calls weren't going to answer themselves.

The first two were easy. Follow-ups on a couple of small burglary cases. Both recently solved. He scheduled a date and time for his range qualifications test. He'd put it off longer than he should have already. Not that he was worried about the test; he was an excellent marksman. It was just carving out the time from his schedule.

A rap on his open door was followed by "Morning, boss." Deputy Scott Reynolds stood in his doorway.

"Morning, Reynolds."

"You hear about the excitement over at the inn last evening?"

Rob straightened, going instantly on a higher state of alert. "What excitement?"

"Somebody was creeping around the place, peeking in windows apparently."

The last of the messages forgotten, Rob pushed to his feet. "Everyone okay?" The image of Grace and her little boy formed in his mind, sending him further on edge.

"Yeah, yeah," Reynolds assured him. "Whoever was poking around was long gone when we arrived. Ms. Myers was pretty upset."

"What about the kid?" Rob forced his heart rate to slow. "He okay?" Liam was a cute kid, really cute, and he'd stolen Rob's heart on day one. He really liked that kid. Liked his mom too, but she kept her distance. Rob respected her wishes. Whatever had broken her trust in relationships, he wasn't going to push for answers. If she was interested, she would let him know when she felt comfortable doing so. He could be patient. He'd decided very quickly that she was the sort of woman worth waiting for.

Reynolds nodded. "Apparently he saw the guy. The boy was able to tell us he was tall, wore a beanie and had blue eyes."

Good to know but not particularly helpful when searching for an unknown perp. "No indication the guy tried to break in or took anything?"

Reynolds shook his head. "His footprints showed he moved around to a few windows and came up on the porch. Nothing seemed to have been tampered with. Nothing taken that Ms. Myers noticed." He shrugged. "I asked her about the boy's father. Since nothing was taken, that was my first thought. Maybe the kid's dad showed up unexpectedly, but she said he passed away."

Rob wanted to ask why he hadn't been called, particularly since he was in charge of the security of this community, but he knew the answer. He'd been on the road transporting a violent criminal. He'd volunteered for the job to prevent one of his less experienced deputies from having to do it.

"I should do a follow-up," he announced, feeling the need to see for himself that all was well. "Have a second look around."

Reynolds shrugged. "I parked on the street and hung around until the chef, Diane Franks, arrived. Everything was all quiet, but if you think there's reason for a second look, I can do that now."

Rob grabbed his cap. "Thanks, but I've got it."

He felt bad for not knowing about this already. That traffic situation had caused him to miss the staff meeting. Generally, he would have passed off the call to someone else in order to be at that meeting, but one of the drivers involved had been a friend who had called him directly. That was the other thing about small communities: everyone knew everyone else.

He headed out to his SUV, thankful the windshield was still clear. He'd had a hell of a time removing the crusted ice this morning. Last night's forecast of two inches of snow had turned into four, with a layer of ice mixed in. The roads had been cleared early this morning, but there would still be side streets and roads that were icy. This time of year, sudden winter storms were to be expected but only appreciated by the kids who got a day home from school.

The Lookout Inn, 10:40 a.m.

THE RENTAL LICENSE plates on the vehicles parked in the lot suggested there were guests. Grace had told him she'd had more bookings than expected all year so far. A number of folks who'd lived in this community for the better part of their lives were impressed with what Grace had done with the inn. When she'd bought it two years ago, it had been closed for nearly a decade. No one really expected it to be brought back to life quite so easily or so well. Grace had come in, renovated the place and put it back on the map in record time.

Folks liked her. She was quiet and reserved, but she tirelessly supported the other businesses and worked hard to keep the inn innovative.

He exhaled a big breath, fogging the air, and headed for the front entrance. Rob had asked her out on three occasions, and she'd turned him down. In a nice way, of course. She was always too busy or Liam was not feeling well.

After the last time, Rob had decided to settle for being friends until she was ready for more—which might be never. He hadn't exactly given up on persuading her to give him a shot, but he had opted to continue being patient. She was a really nice person. Didn't hurt that she was pretty gorgeous too and had an adorable kid to boot. He knew nothing about her past relationships, not even about her deceased husband. But he recognized when a history was bad. She would tell him her story when she felt ready. Something else he could wait for.

When Angela, his former fiancée, had left him, he'd rushed back into the dating scene in an effort, he supposed, to prove something. But that had grown old real quick. From there he'd decided to just take his time and see where life took him.

Then he'd met Grace.

He'd had zero interest anywhere else since.

Rob paused at the entrance to the inn's lobby, squared his shoulders, opened the door and walked in. His gaze instantly locked in on the woman behind the registration desk. Long brown hair so light it was almost blonde. She kept it in a braid, and he'd had plenty of fantasies about deconstructing it. Gray eyes and a smile that stole his breath every single time. The fact that she was a looker was great, but it was her gentle spirit and kind heart that really got to him.

Whoever had hurt this woman had been a fool.

"Mr. Pierce, this is your key." Grace smiled as she passed the actual key—not a card—to the new guest. "You are in cabin 10." She gestured toward the dining room. "Take the French doors out onto the terrace and you'll see the cabins."

"Thank you." He glanced at Rob as he moved closer.

"Morning," Rob said.

The older man gave him a nod. "Good morning to you—" he considered Rob's uniform "—Deputy."

"If you need anything," Grace said to the new arrival, "don't hesitate to let me know."

"Will do." Pierce headed for the dining room. At the door, he glanced back, noted that Rob was still watching and gave another nod before continuing on.

Uniforms made some folks uneasy.

Rob turned his attention to the woman watching him expectantly.

"Good morning," she said, her smile not quite as bright as usual.

"Good morning." He leaned against the counter. "I wish you had called me last night." He didn't bother telling her he was miles away and couldn't have helped, because he wanted her to call him in the future—no matter the circumstances. It was selfish of him, he understood that glaring fact, but he wanted her to feel comfortable coming to him with any issue.

She looked away, busied herself with decluttering after checking in her guest. "I honestly wasn't sure what the situation was." Her gaze finally landed on his once more. "Frankly, I was terrified, and my first thought was to call 911."

"I understand. You had every right to be afraid." Except she had never once mentioned—in the year he had known her—being afraid. She'd had a mountain lion lumber into her backyard, more than her share of woodland varmints. Even a bear once. She'd called for whatever help was required and calmly gone about her business. But he supposed none compared to having a man attempting to look inside your home. Humans could be the most dangerous of predators.

"I should see about the lunch menu." She flashed him another visibly lackluster smile.

"Mind if I tag along?" He wasn't walking away that easily.

She hesitated, then shrugged. "Sure. I just need to let Cara know to keep an eye on the desk."

Rob waited where he stood as she headed for her private residence. Cara Gunter was the new assistant Grace had hired. Well, *new* wasn't exactly right. She'd been here three months already. Nice lady. Hailed from Chattanooga originally, with an elderly grandmother here on the mountain. She'd been in Memphis for years until her grandmother grew too feeble to take care of herself and Cara had moved back. Early thirties, like Grace, and very blunt and focused. But Liam really liked her, which was more than half the battle, Grace had insisted when she hired Cara. With a toddler in the mix, running an inn without an assistant would be impossible. The first assistant Grace hired had died in an automobile accident. Both Grace and Liam had been devastated. These mountain roads could be treacherous.

There was also Karl Wilborn, the gardener, and his wife, Paula, the housekeeper. The couple were lifetime residents of the Mountain. Good folks. Diane Franks was a newcomer. She'd run her own catering business in New York before retiring and relocating to Tennessee, and taking the chef job at the inn. She too was a widow, but rumor was she and the new principal at the middle school were getting serious.

When Grace waved at him from the hall beyond the lobby, he headed in that direction, followed her through the massive dining room. The coffee bar had him wishing for another cup. Grace was brilliant with coffee. She mixed blends and added ingredients that made for some seriously good coffee. Her baking skills were nothing to scoff at either. He'd never been a pastry man, but he dropped by a couple of times a week for Grace's coffee and pastries...and maybe just to say hello.

"Try the new wake-you-up breakfast blend." She gestured to one of the silver coffee urns. "I think it's my best yet."

"I'm always happy to be a taste tester." He picked up one of the dainty china cups and filled it with the steaming brew. "If you ever start your own coffee company, I'm ready to join your staff." He lifted the cup to his lips. The robust but creamy taste burst on his tongue. "Very good."

She smiled. "Thank you."

The aroma of baked scones and muffins lingered in the kitchen. The baskets covered with tea towels he noticed at the coffee bar had likely been loaded with both. His gut rumbled, warning that he should have grabbed breakfast this morning. Wouldn't have mattered, he imagined. Even if he'd already eaten, he would've been lured by Grace's creations.

He'd been invited to Sunday lunch or dinner more

than once. Funny, he'd thought those invitations were leading them in the right direction, but so far that was where things stalled.

"Grab a scone," she suggested, her smile a real one this time. "There's cranberry-orange and cherry."

"They smell great," he said. He set the cup he'd emptied on the counter and went for a cherry scone. He bit off a piece and groaned in satisfaction. "Wow. This is great." He leaned against the counter and, before going for another bite, said, "Tell me about last night."

"It was the end of a busy four-day weekend," she said as she picked up her iPad and checked the screen.

He had learned that Grace kept her menus and other inn-related activities electronically. Made sense, he supposed. But he suspected she studied it now to avoid his gaze. That was off somehow. She'd seemed to trust him well enough. Was comfortable with him as long as he wasn't asking her on a date. Maybe last night had unnerved her more than usual.

"By the time the last guests checked out, I was exhausted." She held her iPad against her chest like a shield now. "Liam had already fallen asleep for a late nap, so I decided to lie down next to him just for a few minutes. I hadn't really meant to drift off, but I did. I woke up an hour or so later, and he was gone from the bed. The house was dark by then, so I went through the house turning on lights and calling his name." She shivered. "The more I called without getting an answer, the more terrified I grew."

He could see how that was a lot scarier than a

mountain lion. "I'm glad you found him and he was okay."

She nodded. "He was in the lobby staring out one of the windows. It was…" She shrugged. "A bit creepy."

He could understand that. "Did Liam say anything?" Rob resisted the urge to reach out and touch her, maybe comfort her. But she wouldn't want him feeling protective. Grace Myers was far too independent.

"He said he was watching the man in the snow." She closed her eyes a moment as if the memory pained her. "The snow had started to fall after I went to sleep, I guess. There was enough by the time I woke up to see the footprints the guy left. I guess the part that really got to me was the idea that anything could have happened to Liam while I was sleeping. I shouldn't have allowed myself to fall asleep like that."

Rob straightened away from the counter. Again, he resisted the urge to reach out. "Have you noticed anyone hanging around or maybe driving by regularly? Since nothing was taken last night, this could be someone casing the place. It's a nice inn. He may believe you keep cash on the premises, and with the inn relatively secluded, it would make for an easy target."

She turned her attention back to the iPad. "No. I haven't noticed anyone hanging around or driving by. Honestly, I'm hoping it was just some person who…" She shrugged. "Who got disoriented in the snow and made a mistake."

It happened, he'd give her that, but the idea was a stretch. "If you think of anything or anyone we should look into, let me know and I'll see that it gets done."

Again, she hugged her iPad. "I will, of course."

She was nervous, but this was more than just the jitters. Talking about what had happened got under her skin. This was a new reaction. One he hadn't seen in Grace before. Maybe it was only because she'd felt Liam had been at risk.

Rob opted to change the subject. "You have more guests coming in this week?"

"The two today and no one else before Friday." She visibly relaxed with the subject change. "I'm very pleased with how the winter business has panned out so far. If the spring and summer carry through with no mechanical breakdowns or bizarre accidents, I think I can safely say we've survived the typical restart costs."

The chamber of commerce had already presented Grace with the best new business award. He expected that was only the first of many honors for her hard work and commitment to the community.

"I've always thought you were going to do well. You're good at the online reach. That's really important for an independent inn like this one."

"I try," she agreed.

The few seconds of silence that lapsed warned that she was ready for him to be on his way. She didn't generally give off that vibe. Obviously she really was rattled.

"If you need me to talk to Liam or anything else, all you have to do is say the word."

She nodded. "And I appreciate that more than you can know."

Another few seconds of silence. Definitely his cue to go. "All right, then. If you don't mind, I'll have a quick look around outside before I head out."

"Sure. That would be great. An extra pair of eyes is always appreciated."

"If I find anything, I'll check back in with you before I go."

She kept a smile in place as she nodded her understanding, but again, it didn't make the usual cut.

He left through the back door.

Maybe her chilly response to him wasn't about what had happened. Could be something else going on. Had she met someone? Had she decided she didn't want to be friends anymore?

Kicking aside the ridiculous and immature ideas, he focused on what he'd promised to do. Taking his time, he walked the shrub border that outlined the perimeter of the backyard. He had a look under the larger shrubs and inside the one good-sized storage shed out back. The door was unlocked, and he'd have to suggest that she keep the building locked going forward. He found nothing unexpected among the yard and gardening tools neatly stored there. Wilborn likely was in and out of the building more than Grace. He'd mention it to the older man as well.

Heading back around front, he spotted Liam at the window. The boy waved. Rob smiled and waved back. He should have insisted on speaking to the boy. Maybe he'd come by later and broach the idea.

Cara, Grace's assistant, appeared behind Liam, gave Rob a wave and then ushered Liam from the window.

All appeared to be good to go. Except he had a gut feeling that something was off with Grace.

He just had no clue what.

Chapter Three

Grace watched from a front window as Rob Vaughn drove away. Her heart reacted with a heavy thud to the idea that she should have been truthful with him. Maybe it was time she told someone the whole story. Particularly after last night.

But if she did, she risked her identity and location getting out. She could not—would not—risk Liam's safety by allowing anyone to know the truth.

Not even the man she had come to trust…had come to have feelings for.

So not smart, Grace.

She shivered, hugged her arms around herself. She should have learned her lesson three years ago.

Didn't matter. Rob Vaughn would never know how she felt. He would—could—never know her secrets. How could she possibly ever have any sort of deeper relationship with anyone while keeping the kind of secrets she could never ever share?

She couldn't.

"Diane says lunch is ready if you'd like to join us."

Cara's voice startled Grace. She ushered her thoughts

back to the present and smiled at her assistant. "Thank you, Cara. I'll be right there."

Cara nodded and walked away. Grace wasn't sure what she would do without the woman. She'd felt torn about the need for an assistant when she'd hired Cara. Kendall Walls had been with her from the time she moved to the Mountain. Kendall was the daughter of the assistant who had worked with the former owners back when the inn was in operation. The previous owners had highly recommended her. Grace and Liam had adored her. The accident and losing her still hurt. It wasn't until nearly two months later that Grace had been forced to break down and hire someone else. She just hadn't been able to handle everything alone and take care of Liam.

The holiday season had blasted off, and Liam was getting so independent. He wasn't always agreeable to following Mommy around and entertaining himself with his toys. Neither of which was a bad thing, except she couldn't watch him as closely as she preferred.

Plus Grace so loved baking. Without help, she couldn't possibly do much of her own baking. So, she'd started the interviewing process and found Cara. With her housekeeper and gardener and the wondrous chef, Diane Franks, they had made it through the holiday season without a glitch.

Grace added more logs to the fire. She adored the inglenook-style fireplace. She was so grateful that it hadn't been closed in or altered during the numerous renovations that had come before. Most of the inn was heated by a modern gas system, including a neat little fireplace in each guest room. But this large one in the lobby was completely original.

The sound of her little boy's voice had her smiling as she moved toward the dining room. Liam was already entertaining whoever had decided to pop in for lunch. All the way from Seattle was Henry Brower, sixtyish, with salt-and-pepper hair and kind eyes, who sat at the far end of the table. He was laughing at something Liam had said or done. Cara sat next to Liam. Their other guest, Joe Pierce, from Los Angeles, had not come inside, yet Grace hoped he would put in an appearance. She enjoyed chatting with her guests. To Grace, part of the draw of inns and bed-and-breakfasts was the gathering for meals. She had altered her appearance enough to do so without worry of being recognized. That too was something she had worried about in the beginning. But in two years no one had recognized her, so she'd begun to relax…until last night.

Henry smiled in Grace's direction when she picked up a plate at the serving buffet. With effort, she returned the smile before surveying the lovely meal Diane had prepared. An array of sandwiches and a very tasty-looking salad. Grace had baked a variety of cookies. Chocolate with walnuts and drizzled with white icing, cherry almond with sprinkles, and lemon with white chocolate. Diane had arranged them beautifully on a vintage tray. Grace was thankful for the vintage dinnerware and serving pieces. It felt important to the atmosphere she wanted to create—something she and the previous owners shared. Guests frequently complimented the choices.

Funny how a small compliment could go so far after all she'd been through these past few years. In her old life, she had been an accountant. She'd worked for a large firm with an enviable salary and great benefits. But the environment had been cold and austere. It had been nothing like owning and operating an inn.

Grace moved to the table and sat down beside her little boy. He was busy telling Mr. Brower all about last night's excitement. Grace bit back the urge to hush him. It was too late anyway.

"Was this a ghost you saw?" Brower asked, his eyes big with feigned concern.

Liam moved his head somberly from side to side. "No. It was a scary man."

Grace patted Liam on the back. "But he's gone now," she assured him.

Liam nodded and took another bite of his peanut butter and jelly sandwich. He pointed a finger at Brower. "Mommy says he's *neber* coming back."

"I am so glad to hear that," Brower affirmed.

Cara looked to Grace. She kept a smile in place for her assistant. Cara had seemed inordinately worried about Grace when they talked this morning. Cara often voiced her concerns about Grace and Liam being here alone at night when there were no guests. The closest neighbors were nearly a mile down the lane. But Grace hadn't worried—at least, not until last night. Still, she wasn't sharing that worry with Cara.

The memory of Liam describing the man's eyes as being like his had her quivering deep inside where no one could see.

Liam had his father's eyes.

Grace pushed away the thought.

"Mr. Brower, what brings you to our mountain?" Cara asked.

Brower sipped his iced tea. "I'm here for a mini conference in Chattanooga. I prefer the peace and quiet of a small community like this rather than staying downtown amid the hustle and bustle."

"We appreciate your choosing our inn," Grace said.

The middle set of French doors that led onto the terrace opened and Mr. Pierce appeared, aiming straight for the serving buffet. He was perhaps mid-fifties, with a shaved head that contrasted sharply with his long beard. He'd arrived this morning. Grace was always unsettled when a guest from California arrived. She wasn't sure she would ever get past worrying if that person had seen her ex-husband in person…or perhaps had seen Grace. She'd gone to great lengths to avoid being recognized. She wore her hair longer now, and darker. She worked diligently to keep her blond roots covered.

Changing hers and Liam's names had been the most difficult part. Finding the right sort of help—someone who did foolproof work—to pull off new IDs wasn't as easy as the movies made it seem. When she'd started her business here at the inn, she had taken the sole proprietorship route—far less complicated. Thankfully, her son had been only an infant when they'd had to disappear. With her father's death, there was no one left behind to consider. Her few close friends and old acquaintances likely no longer missed her. He had ensured she'd distanced herself from basically everyone during those final months together. She'd had no idea how much he'd controlled her life until it was too late.

Sadly, that had been a mistake, as was every other decision she had made after meeting Adam Locke.

She glanced down at her precious son. Except for sweet Liam. She could never regret him or the nightmare she had survived to have him.

"I should get back to work." Cara rose from her chair, plate and glass in hand, and hurried from the dining room.

"Mr. Pierce," Grace said, acknowledging the new arrival despite her reservations, "I hope your cabin is satisfactory."

He settled at the table, directly across from her. "It's great. Everything is great." He said the last with a lingering glance at Liam.

"This is my son," she said, "Liam." She smiled when Liam looked up. "Liam, this is Mr. Pierce."

Liam gave a salute. This was something new he'd picked up from his most beloved cartoon.

Pierce gave an indifferent nod before turning his attention to his salad.

When Liam had lost interest in the remainder of his lunch, Grace ushered him from the table, gathering their plates and glasses.

"Have a nice afternoon, gentlemen," she offered. "Please let me know if you need anything."

Liam skipped along beside her until they reached the kitchen. Diane had left already since she also taught an afternoon yoga class. She would be back in time to take care of dinner. Judging by the delicious scent filling the room, Grace suspected there was a roast in the oven. No one made a better or more tender roast than Diane.

While Liam created a Lego tower on the rug, Grace inventoried the pantry and refrigerator. She added the items that needed to be restocked to the list Diane had made for the upcoming week's meals. Grace placed the order online, and Diane would pick it up on her way back to the inn this evening. Now that the guests had left the dining room, Grace cleared the lunch service and settled the glass dome back over the cookies. Those would stay handy in the event a guest needed a snack.

Once Grace had loaded the dishwasher, she and Liam retired to their space for his nap. She generally used the time for catching up on paperwork. As she settled on the sofa, she heard the vacuum running in the lobby. Paula Wilborn, the housekeeper, had arrived. She'd needed the morning off for an appointment. With Paula here, her husband would be about, clearing pathways or raking leaves. The couple was very good at their work and needed no direction, something Grace was grateful for.

Liam took a few extra minutes to settle. Last night's excitement still had him wound up. When he'd finally fallen asleep, Grace dared to start the search she'd been dreading. She'd resisted the idea last night, this morning as well. It was easy to pretend she was too busy to take a moment. But the truth was, she was terrified at what she would find.

Stop. Adam was in jail. His trial had started at the beginning of the month. Or at least that was the last information she'd found. Trial dates were subject to numerous sorts of changes. The original trial date had been set only months after his arrest—two years ago. But then there had been countless delays. Scheduling issues with attorneys. There was discovery and depositions and much preparation that led to many requests for continuances. On and on it had gone. Once the trial actually started, it was expected to take several weeks, perhaps a couple of months, just because of the sheer number of witnesses and the mountain of evidence.

Grace's statement had been videotaped. She did not have to testify again. At least, that was the promise. Didn't matter now. After her father's sudden death, she had made the decision to disappear. No one knew where she was or how to contact her. She might not have made the decision if not for the fact that her testimony was barely a sliver of what the DA had against the bastard. If for some unforeseeable reason they wanted her to make an appearance and couldn't reach her, it wouldn't make or break the case.

The evidence actually spoke for itself.

Nothing could change Adam's destiny now.

She stalled, fingers poised on the keyboard. Every time she thought about him and about the trial, she found herself back in that crazy loop of fear and self-loathing. How had she lived in that house for all those months and not known what Adam had in his secret basement room?

The hot, sour taste that rose in her mouth had her lunch threatening to make a reappearance. She closed her eyes, swallowed back the bitterness and forced herself to calm. She was away from him now. He would never see his son...would never touch his son.

But what if the blue-eyed man from last night had been him?

No. No. No. It couldn't have been. There had to be a reasonable explanation.

Gathering her resolve, she opened her eyes and forced herself to type the name.

Adam Locke.

Grace held her breath while the search results populated her screen.

Locke Case Thrown Out on Technicality...police must start from scratch...

For several seconds her brain refused to absorb the meaning behind the words.

She swallowed back the lump in her throat and compelled herself to continue reading.

The San Francisco District Attorney's Office had been hiding a secret—the warrant used to obtain the majority of the evidence against the Sweetheart Killer, Adam Locke, contained a fatal flaw. The warrant authorizing lead investigator Detective Lance Gibbons to search the suspect's home was not obtained until after the forced entry into the Locke residence. Since exigent circumstances could not be proved, the search of the Locke property was unlawful. The judge's decision suppresses all evidence found in the unlawful search of the home.

Ice filling her veins, Grace's gaze zoomed back up to the top of the article to see when it was released.

Friday.

Which meant Adam could have been here last night.

Fear tightened her chest, wrapped around her throat like bony fingers.

This couldn't be right. No. Not possible.

Okay, okay. He was out. There was no denying this. The words were right in front of her. Still, wouldn't the investigation resume? Wouldn't he be under house arrest or something like that under the circumstances? The man was definitely a flight risk.

And even if for some reason he had ditched the house arrest ankle bracelet or whatever, how would he have known where to find her?

The same way you escaped with a new, fake ID.

Anything was possible if a person was willing to pay the price.

Hands shaking, Grace closed the search box. No, she refused to live in fear again. He couldn't possibly know where she was. Finding her wouldn't have been that easy. But he had… To deny it was ridiculous. Still, how had he managed the feat in less than forty-eight hours?

Unless he'd had someone looking for her all this time.

She shook her head. Stood on shaky legs. She'd been too careful. So, so careful.

Grace hurried, her feet tripping over each other, to the bedroom to see her son. He slept like an angel in the middle of the big down comforter. Her heart ached at the idea that her child would never be free if that bastard was out there.

Her heart stumbled, flailed like a wounded bird. Adam would do all in his power to kill her. She was the reason he had been caught. She was the one who'd told Detective Gibbons about the room in the basement. She was the one to release his final victim, and still the woman had somehow managed to get murdered. If that last victim had lived, she could have testified about what Adam had done.

Grace should have done more…should have found a way to save her.

She lowered herself onto the side of the bed. She hadn't witnessed her husband kidnapping or harming anyone. He'd been so charming, so good to her. She would never have known about any of it if she hadn't found that room.

How had she not sensed the evil in him?

After what she'd found, she had gone straight to her father in Lake Tahoe. Together they had come up with a plan that would best protect Grace and the child she carried. She had called the hotline for the Sweetheart Killer. Instantly she had been connected with the lead detective—Lance Gibbons. She'd told him everything she knew. All the police had to do was go to Adam's place of employment and take him in for questioning, obtain a search warrant for their home, and voilà—he would spend the rest of his life in prison because of what he'd done.

Adam Locke—her husband, her son's father—had been a serial killer.

Grace inhaled a deep breath, then another to slow her runaway heart. She had to think clearly—something she hadn't done then.

Her husband had come home that evening and discovered his house had been invaded by the San Francisco Police Department, so he'd driven right on by and gone straight to her father's house. The bastard had known that if the police had found him there was only one person to blame. And he'd known exactly where she'd gone.

He had driven the two hundred miles from San Francisco to Lake Tahoe. She and her father had no idea the police had not taken him into custody. No one bothered to call with the warning. This, she now realized, was where the detectives had jumped the gun. Rather than going to Adam's workplace and arresting him, they'd gone to the house and burst through the door to get their hands on the evidence first. They had claimed she told them there could be a victim in jeopardy in the basement. And she had, sort of. She'd released the victim she'd found, but certainly her husband could have brought in another as soon as Grace left. It wasn't like she had set out to mislead the police. How was she supposed to have known what his schedule was like? She hadn't even known he was a killer. Damn it.

Not to mention she had been confused and terrified…out of her mind, really.

But she hadn't claimed with any certainty that there was another victim in the basement and some ambitious clerk had zeroed in on that discrepancy in her statement during the latest deep dig into the evidence. After all those months of preparation for trial, it was all for naught because of one five-letter word.

Might.

In her answer to the question of whether or not there may have been yet another victim stashed somewhere in the house, she had stated there *might* be. Because like everyone else in the tristate area, she'd been aware that another woman fitting the profile of his victims had recently gone missing. Bella Watts. To Grace's knowledge, she was never found.

While the police had conducted what was now considered an illegal search and seizure, Adam had broken into her father's home to get to her. He'd left her father unconscious on the floor and chased her through the snowy woods behind the family cabin. Her water had broken during the chase, and she'd thought for certain both she and her baby were dead. After he'd found her waving for help on the side of the road, she rushed back into the woods and he'd abandoned the car and followed. He'd had her on the ground, choking her, when her hand found that rock. She'd slammed it into his head. When he toppled off her, she scrambled up and ran. She had hoped the blow killed him. Later, at the hospital, after Liam was born, she and her father had learned that his body had not been found.

Adam Locke was gone.

Two days later, sitting in a chair next to her hospital bed, her father had suffered a fatal heart attack in his sleep.

She'd named her son after him, William James. Weeks later, with her husband finally arrested in an attempt to get to her and Liam, she had made up her mind that the police would never be able to keep her safe. She'd taken her father's insurance money and savings and disappeared.

She hadn't cared if the police believed her dead— that was all the better. Adam Locke had not just fans but followers, Gibbons had told her, who looked up to him. Any one of them would have loved to see her dead. She suspected he had told her this to keep her pliable, but all he'd done was make her more determined and given her all the more reason to disappear.

Grace forced the horrible memories away. She checked the windows before leaving the room but didn't close the door. If a sound came from where her son lay sleeping, she wanted to know.

Her fingers itched to pick up the phone and call Detective Gibbons. He could tell her what was really happening. But she couldn't risk her call being traced. He would want her to return to San Francisco. Though he

A Place to Hide

had her videotaped testimony, he would no doubt feel that an in-person statement would serve the case better.

She couldn't do it. Not and risk Liam's life. Not for anything.

The best thing to do was to stay calm. No one here knew she was Gianna Locke. Liam's California birth certificate carried the name Aidan Reinhart Locke—the name she and Adam had chosen. She had only used that name in an attempt to prevent him from ever knowing the real name she intended to give her son, William James Myers. She had gone way back in her mother's family history to find the name Myers. Grace was an easy decision since it was no doubt by the grace of God that she and Liam had escaped the bastard.

A rap on the door of their private quarters had her hurrying there. She needed Liam's nap to last long enough for her to consider what steps she might need to take.

She opened the door to find Cara.

"I'm sorry, but I need to leave early today. Is that a problem?"

"Go ahead." Grace took a deep breath. "I can monitor the lobby from here until Liam wakes up." Her door had a direct view into the lobby.

Cara smiled. "Thanks. I appreciate it. My grandmother has an appointment with her heart specialist, and she failed to tell me until a few minutes ago."

"No worries. You take care of your grandmother. We'll be fine here."

Grace left the door open and watched as Cara exited through the main entrance. She wondered if the woman had any idea how lucky she was to still have family alive. Grace had Liam and she cherished him beyond measure, but she missed her father so desperately. Her mother had died when Grace was only five years old, and since Grace had been an only child, there was no other family. Her parents had no siblings either, so she truly was alone except for Liam. She had always told herself she would never have an only child for just that reason, but now she couldn't see herself ever trusting anyone enough to go down that path again.

The image of Rob Vaughn slipped into her mind, but she dismissed it. He was a very nice man, but no matter how much she liked him, and he appeared to like her, his opinion of her would change dramatically when he learned the truth. Considering what she had just discovered, she wasn't sure how long her dark secret would stay hidden.

Rob had family. He would never dream of bringing someone with her past into that tight, loving group. It was foolish even to consider such an idea. He deserved someone without the sort of baggage she carried.

The front entrance opened, and Grace's heart stopped. Why hadn't she locked it after Cara left?

Because she had guests. She couldn't lock the door until tonight.

Cara. It was Cara coming back. Grace managed to breathe again.

"Did you forget something?"

"The mail." She placed it on the desk. "See you tomorrow." She waved and disappeared out the door once more.

Grace steadied herself. She had to pull herself together. She had a son who needed her, and she had guests. She couldn't fret about this a minute longer. She had to do something. If she worked at the desk, at least that would put her between the front door and Liam. First, she popped into the kitchen and ensured the back door was locked. Diane had a key. No need to leave it unlocked.

The inn was quiet with only two guests and Liam having a nap. The only sound was the big old grandfather clock ticking. There were many vintage clocks throughout the inn, but the grandfather clock in the lobby was her favorite. The sound soothed her just a little.

At the desk, she checked her email. Worked hard to keep her mind off events in California. Then she picked up the bundle of mail and picked through it.

The utility bill sat on top. She opened it, reviewed the charges, then set it aside. She would take it to her desk later. Then she smiled when she counted three postcards from previous guests who wanted to thank her again for a lovely stay. She appreciated the online reviews, but to receive a handwritten note was particularly heartwarming.

A copy of the *Lookout Mountain Monitor*. She set it aside as well to review later with a cup of tea. It was her favorite late-afternoon appointment with herself. Lots of junk mail, which she tossed into the recycle bin beneath the desk. A six-by-nine-inch white envelope with no markings. A frown tugged at her brow. Probably went with the junk mail, but she checked to see what was inside just in case.

A photograph…the kind printed from a computer onto plain white paper.

She froze, then started to shake as her heart bumped back into rhythm and then began to pound frantically.

Liam…standing at that window last evening. His curly blond hair sleep tousled.

Someone had taken the picture from outside the window. The man Liam had seen in the snow.

The man with blue eyes like Liam's.

"Oh my God."

He was here.

Grace didn't have to wonder. Adam had signed the bottom of the photograph the way he always signed notes to her.

XOXO

Chapter Four

Bluebird Trail, 1:30 p.m.

"Mrs. Sells, you're certain about the timing?"

Rob watched the elderly woman consider the question. She'd called to say someone had been staying in her garage. From the looks of the place, someone had indeed fashioned a makeshift bed by throwing together a couple of moving quilts in one corner.

"Well, I was out here Sunday around lunchtime. I parked my car in the garage after church, so I think I would have seen this mess then."

Rob nodded. "But you haven't been out here since then?"

"Not until lunch today," she explained. "Mattie England and I have lunch together every Monday. I didn't notice anything out of place until I came back, of course. When the garage door opened I could see straight in here and there it was." She shook her head. "Now, I don't mind anyone trying to stay warm by whatever means is handy, but it would be nice to be warned."

Rob gave the lady a nod. "Mrs. Sells, if someone you don't know shows up at your house needing a warm place to stay, you send them on over to the shelter on Bennett Street. There's always plenty of room there. Never let a stranger into your house."

"Well, now, Deputy," she argued, "he didn't knock on my door."

Okay, now Rob was really worried. "Did you see this man?"

The ninety-year-old lady frowned. "Well, no, but I did see a young fella walking down the trail just before dark on Sunday. He wasn't from around here, so I suspect he's the culprit who did this." She gestured to the mound in front of her vintage Ford sedan. "No one who lives in the neighborhood would do this and then not bother to fold the quilts up and put them away like he found them. He could have at least done that."

"What was this man wearing?" Rob asked, pulling out his notepad to jot down anything she remembered. Under other circumstances the lady's opinion might have been amusing, but these days nothing about an intruder should be minimized.

"A black coat and one of those beanie things." She patted her head. "It was black too."

The man Liam had seen had been wearing a beanie. Considering Bluebird Trail was the next street over from Mockingbird Lane, there was a reasonable possibility it was the same guy.

"Could you see any details of his face? Was he Caucasian?"

"Oh, yes, yes, he was. I couldn't make out any real details like the size of his nose or anything like that, but it was clear that he was white."

Rob surveyed the garage again. "Have you noticed anything missing? Tools? Anything at all?"

"Well, no." She too glanced around. "But I never really kept up with what Harvey had in here. The garage was his domain."

Harvey was her late husband. He'd passed away last year.

"Do you mind if I have a look around?"

"You go right ahead, Deputy." She shivered. "I'm going in the house. It's cold out here with that overhead door open."

"Yes, ma'am, you do that. I'll close the door and check in with you before I leave."

When the lady had gone back into the house, Rob started on one side of the garage and surveyed the shelves. Tools lined most of them. Tools for working on automobiles and tools for gardening. Since Mrs. Sells rarely came into the garage, he hoped anything recently taken or moved would be noticeable due to the fine layer of dust that coated the shelves. He moved slowly along one side, then progressed to the other. Nothing jumped out at him. He retraced his steps, studying the concrete floor where a few items were stored beneath the shelves. In the corner, sawhorses had been tucked away. A creeper for sliding beneath cars. None of which appeared to have been moved.

So far, it seemed that whoever had found his way

into the Sells garage had only been looking for a place to sleep. Still, this was not safe, particularly for an elderly person like Mrs. Sells.

Rob closed up the garage and walked to the back door of the Sells home. He knocked and then waited for the lady to answer.

She opened the door. "Did you find anything?"

"No, ma'am, nothing more than you did." He made a face. "I'm not happy with the idea of someone creeping about on your property. I need you to be sure to keep your doors locked at all times. Tonight, around six, I or another deputy will come by and check your garage. We'll do it again at midnight. If you have no objections, we'll do this for a couple of days just to be sure he's gone for good. If your trespasser notices this, he may find someplace new to hang out."

"Sounds like a good plan," she agreed.

"But I do need you to call it in if you see any strangers in the area. Even if they're just on the street. If someone you don't recognize is walking by, I want to hear about it." This was a dead-end street with little or no traffic. Strangers stood out.

"I sure will," she promised.

"All right, then. I'll be on my way."

Rob had just backed out of the Sells drive when his cell sounded off.

Grace Myers.

His pulse rate sped up as he accepted the call. "Hey, Grace. Everything okay?"

"There was something in my mail," she said, her

tone more than a little reluctant. "Do you mind dropping by and having a look?"

"I'll be right there."

Mockingbird Lane, 2:10 p.m.

WHILE LIAM RAN around the room chasing the multicolored balls that had escaped his portable ball pit, his mom stood by nervously watching Rob study the photograph and envelope she'd discovered in her mailbox.

Since there was no address and no postage mark, obviously the envelope had been placed in her mailbox by someone unaffiliated with the postal service. Also, obviously, it was the person who had walked through the snow and stood on her porch staring through a window at her son.

He hated to ask the question he couldn't avoid any longer. It would sound like an accusation, and he didn't want that. But there was no way around it. "And you don't have any idea who may have left this for you to find?"

It was the lengthy hesitation before she summoned a response that told him all he needed to know.

"I—I just can't imagine why anyone would do this." She gestured to the photo. "It makes no sense."

Rob glanced at Liam to ensure he was occupied with his attempts to get all the balls back into the pit before saying what he could no longer put off. "Think carefully about your answer, Grace. This person could be dangerous. You shouldn't have any hesitation talking to me about this. The *XOXO* at the bottom feels personal."

Tears welled in her eyes, and she blinked rapidly to hold them back. "Give me a minute."

She hurried into the hall outside her private parlor and called for Mrs. Wilborn. A moment later the housekeeper appeared, and Grace asked her to stay with Liam for a bit. Evidently, whatever Grace had to talk about, she didn't want Liam overhearing.

Mrs. Wilborn smiled as she breezed into the small parlor. "Afternoon, Deputy Vaughn."

"Afternoon, Mrs. Wilborn. How's Mr. Wilborn?"

She harrumphed. "Complaining as always but managing to stay out of trouble."

Rob laughed. "Planning that big garden already, I imagine."

"He is." She settled on the floor with Liam. "What's happening here, Mr. Liam?"

Grace waited in the doorway. "We can talk in the kitchen."

Rob gave her a nod and followed her in that direction.

In the kitchen, he waited while Grace opened one cabinet door after the other. He had no idea what she was searching for or why, so he settled on a stool at the island and waited patiently.

"Finally," she said, withdrawing something from the last cupboard she searched. She set a fifth of bourbon on the counter, then went to another cupboard and grabbed two glasses. She placed them next to the bottle, opened it and poured a generous serving in each glass.

She looked to him. Blinked. "Sorry, I didn't think to ask if you cared to join me. I just assumed." She passed a glass to him, then raised her own and drank deeply.

His eyebrows reared up in surprise. This was going to be interesting. He'd never seen Grace drink wine or beer, much less anything stronger. Rather than explain how he was on duty, he simply set the glass down and waited for her to spill whatever was troubling her. The quickest way to slow the momentum of someone who wanted to talk was to make some unrelated comment.

Her glass landed on the counter once more and the look of pain on her face told him he was right to assume she wasn't much of a drinker. When she finally managed to swallow the strong liquid, she cleared her throat, coughed, cleared her throat again and managed a breath.

"Better now?" he asked.

She shuddered a little. "We'll see."

He felt confident this was no time to laugh, but he couldn't resist a soft chuckle. "Want to tell me what this is all about?"

GRACE CONSIDERED POURING another deep shot of bourbon but figured she should stop while she was ahead. Otherwise she might not be able to stay standing. She couldn't take that risk no matter how much she would love to drown out the world for a little while.

Keeping Liam safe was all that mattered. Not her feelings. Not her own safety—only his.

Which was why she had to do this. There was no pretending it would all be okay. Not anymore. Her reprieve from the nightmare was over.

For more than two years she had promised herself that no one would ever know the truth about her past. No one would ever hear the awful story and associate Liam or her with it. But she had no choice now.

Clearly the legal system had failed Liam. Failed her. Failed all those victims.

She squared her shoulders, stared Rob Vaughn straight in the eyes and said what she needed to say. "I'm not who you think I am."

There. She'd said it. She allowed herself to breathe again. The burn in her throat and stomach had settled, and she felt the beginnings of another sort of warmth seeping through her system.

"Can you be a bit more specific?"

He frowned, his brown eyes clouding with questions. He had the nicest brown eyes and thick black hair.

She blinked. *Focus, Grace.*

When she failed to find the words to continue in a timely manner, he said, "I can see this is serious." He nodded to her. "You're serious."

"Yes. Very serious. My real name is Gianna Reinhart Locke. You may have heard of my…" *Take a deep breath and just say it.* "My ex-husband is Adam Locke."

He didn't have to say a word. The look on his face

told her that he knew who she meant. The whole world knew.

She closed her eyes and forced away the memories that attempted to intrude.

"Okay."

The single word caused her lids to flutter open. She studied his face. She had come to trust this man on some level. Something she had thought she would never again do. She liked him. Was attracted to him. And he felt the same way about her. But now, the way he looked at her put a new fracture in her already damaged heart. He didn't look at her with suspicion but with something far too similar, and it hurt. It hurt because she had worked so hard to build a new life here. She had struggled and fought to make it the best life possible for her and her son.

Now it was all crashing down.

"I barely got away from him after..." She forced her mind to allow the past back in. She had kept it at bay for so long that her brain resisted the intrusion now. "That day..." The memory of that day—the hours that bled into night. "I discovered the basement room that morning. He'd left extra early for work. He was supposed to be on vacation, but an emergency had come up and he'd had to go into the office."

The man she had married—the man she had thought she knew better than herself—had been a savvy businessman. He'd traveled frequently. But twice a year he had taken a week off. Grace hadn't known then what the timing was all about. Most people she knew took a vacation once a year. But not Adam. Every six months he took a week off. He stayed home and worked on his projects.

She, like a good wife, had believed him. Just as she had believed his projects were the handmade furniture he crafted for their home and as gifts for special friends. His little semiannual vacations were always spent on his *projects*. The two of them never actually went on a vacation. This hadn't bothered her at the time because they'd only been married a few months before she'd gotten pregnant, and then they'd both wanted to stay near home.

"He was angry," she continued, her voice sounding hollow. She hugged her arms around herself as the memories and the cold that accompanied them filled her. "It was some sort of emergency with an account, and he was livid that he had to go into the office on his time off." She vividly recalled how furious he'd been. "The baby was due in a short two weeks, and his big surprise was not finished." Her mouth struggled with forming the words she had to say. "He warned me not to go into the basement. He said I might fall and he didn't want me to see his surprise until it was finished."

She hadn't meant to break her promise. She really hadn't. "I never went into the basement. It was his domain. I thought it was a bit odd that he pressed me on the issue that morning." She fell silent for a moment. "But not long after he left I started to understand."

She looked around the kitchen she loved so much. Nothing would ever be the same now. "At first I thought I left the television on in the bedroom. But

I hadn't and then I heard the sound again. A banging or thudding from the basement somewhere."

When she didn't continue, he prodded, "What did you do next?"

She blinked, drew back from the memory. If she allowed herself to be too fully immersed, she would never get this told. "I got up and checked the house. The doors and windows were locked. There was no one in the house except me. No one in the yard. I even considered that I'd imagined it or maybe that a bird had somehow gotten trapped in the attic. Then the sound grew louder, more frantic, and I realized it wasn't in the attic."

She moistened her lips. "I took a hammer from the drawer in the kitchen where we kept miscellaneous items." She shrugged. "We all have one of those drawers." She thought of the one by the back door in this very kitchen. "I unlocked the basement door." She frowned, considered that the locked door needed additional explanation. "The door to the basement was in the hall, and Adam had insisted on keeping it locked. Since the stairs led right up to the door, I figured he didn't want a guest—not that we actually had people over—to think they were walking into a bathroom and fall down the stairs. It made sense to me at the time."

Rob nodded. "I can see that."

She tried to smile, couldn't. "I turned on the hall light and started down the stairs. The banging was so much louder down there." She recalled how her heart had started to pound in time with the banging. Fear had pumped through her veins.

"I told myself that maybe there was an animal trapped down there…but even then I had started to realize something was very, very wrong." When she reached the bottom of the stairs, she flipped the switch turning on the overhead fixture. "When I turned on the light the banging stopped. Almost like whatever it was knew someone was there and was afraid of who it might be."

The quaking started deep inside her as if she were there now, standing in the middle of that basement with the knowledge that something was terribly wrong welling inside her. It had been the strongest, most crushing sensation—a knowing that whatever came next was going to change everything.

"The cradle in the center of the room, amid his tools, stole my attention for a moment." Pride and happiness had swelled inside her. So that was his surprise. A cradle for the baby. She hadn't known. "For just a moment I was so happy." The ache in her chest was fierce, as if the memory were only yesterday. "Then the banging started again. This time there was grunting…some sort of muffled sound."

Grace had moved to the wall where the sound appeared to be coming from. The banging was so loud there it had made her jump.

"At that point, I think I was in a sort of shock. I said, 'Hello? Is someone there?'"

The grunting and nonverbal sounds clearly coming from a person had become so loud that she stumbled back.

Someone was on the other side of that wall.

She had stared at the narrow basement window on each side of the room. The windows were up high near the ceiling and very small. She had closed her eyes a moment and mentally calculated where this first set—in the foundation, one on each side of the house—were located. She had realized then that the wall she stared at was about the center of the house. There could be more basement space beyond it.

"I knew I had to get beyond that wall…because someone was there. I pulled and tugged at the shelving units lining the wall. Things fell off the shelves but I ignored them. I couldn't stop. I had to know… to fix whatever this was." Her pulse bumped into a faster rhythm.

Behind the unit crowded with the most items was a frameless door painted the same color as the wall so that it almost blended in.

"I almost didn't see the door. I remember reaching out…my fingers wrapping around the handle." She made a face. "Even the handle was painted like the wall. I kept thinking how strange it was."

But the door was locked.

"I turned the handle again, and the sounds on the other side grew more frantic. No matter how I tugged and twisted on the handle, it wouldn't open. I said out loud that I was going to find the key. I searched and searched for a key. Every drawer. Every shelf. The whole time questions were pounding in my brain.

Why was someone locked in some sort of room in our basement? What if it was some bad person? Should I call the police?"

She clasped her hands together, pressed them to her lips for a moment before she could go on. "I couldn't find the key. I wrapped my arms protectively around my belly, thinking how I had to be careful because of the baby and wondering what I should do."

If she called the police...

Foolishly, the idea of her husband being taken away had torn at her heart. She had tried to rationalize the situation. If someone was locked in the basement, Adam must have some sort of compelling reason...

No, that made no sense.

"Then I took a deep breath and I knew what I had to do. I wanted to demand answers before I opened that door, but obviously whoever was locked in there couldn't answer since he or she was gagged or something." She shrugged. "I kept thinking that I trusted my husband completely...but this..." She braced her arms on the counter and went on. "I walked over to the door and I said that it sounded as if you've been gagged and you can't speak. The answering sounds were clearly a yes, even though the word wasn't stated. I said I would ask a question and I wanted one bang on the wall for no and two for yes. I asked if that was okay. I got one bang and then another."

Whatever Rob was thinking, he kept his face reasonably neutral. But he watched her so closely...so intently. She could only imagine what he was thinking.

"I first asked if the person was a man. There was one bang, so this was a woman. Then I asked if she was injured. One bang and then another." Even now, Grace's heart pounded even harder with the memories. "Then I asked if a man had put her in there. Two bangs. Still wanting to believe my husband had to be innocent, I asked about his hair color and eye color. By the time I made myself stop, I knew beyond any doubt that Adam was responsible. It took a moment for me to gather my wits, and then I told her I was going to find a way to get her out. I looked around the basement, searching for something usable, and I spotted an axe. I grabbed it and walked back to the door. I told her to stand back."

Grace squeezed her eyes shut at the memory of swinging that axe with all her might.

"When you got her out, did you take her to the hospital or the police?"

The sound of Rob's voice forced her eyes open. "She didn't give me the chance. As soon as I had untied her and removed the gag, she ran out of the house and down the street. I couldn't run after her. I was nine months pregnant. By the time I got the car keys and tried to follow her, she was gone. Then I just started driving. I didn't stop until I reached my father's house in Lake Tahoe."

From there everything had gone downhill.

By the time Grace had told Rob the rest of what had happened that day and then about what she'd learned on the internet, Diane had arrived to prepare the evening meal. He waited patiently while she and

Diane chatted for a moment, then followed her to her private quarters. Mrs. Wilborn hurried back to finish her chores and Liam had fallen asleep during the movie he'd begged to watch.

"I can make some calls," he said. "It's possible Adam was released on bail pending other charges. We can't be sure what actually happened until I speak to the detectives there. What we read in the press is not always completely accurate."

"If Adam's not here," she said, her heart flopping helplessly behind her breastbone, "then someone he sent is here. Either way, my son is not safe. And just like that woman who ran away from my house—Alicia Holder—the police won't be able to protect us. Believe that if you believe nothing else I've told you. He is the worst kind of monster. You have no idea."

Rob nodded. "I have some idea. I followed the story."

Grace felt confident he didn't really understand. He was in law enforcement and had likely seen and heard bad things, but no one save someone who had survived that kind of evil could really understand. Either way, she needed his help. If she could have gotten through this alone, she would never have told him this awful truth. She remembered the locket she'd hidden under the sink… She should turn that over to him. It was evidence, after all. But somehow with all the secrets she'd kept from him already, she just couldn't bring herself to share one more ugly piece of this nightmare. Especially since she hadn't given it to the deputy who'd come last night. Now she just felt ridiculous for not doing so.

"I have to get my son to safety." She braced herself for a battle. "If I simply notify the detectives on his case, then they'll want me to stay put. I can't take that risk."

"What is it you want to do?"

As much as she wanted to trust this man, she wasn't sure she should. He was a cop. He had an obligation to the badge he wore. "All I'm asking is that you let me get my son to someplace safe. If you can't or won't help me, I'm doing it alone. I don't want to risk my son's safety, so I'm begging you, please help me hide him."

He held her gaze for a long moment. "I should say no. I mean, you could have told me this a long time ago. I could have been helping you from day one."

She bit her lips together and prayed he wouldn't allow pride or anger or anything else to sway him.

"But the answer is yes, I'll help you get Liam to safety before I do anything else."

"Thank you." Such relief washed through her she wanted to weep.

"Don't thank me yet. I haven't told you my conditions."

Chapter Five

Rob wasn't entirely confident he'd made the right decision, but more important than anything, he needed her to trust him. For that, he had to at least give her instinct to hide the benefit of the doubt. Protecting her child was top priority—for them both.

No time like the present to jump in.

"First," he said, "I decide the place."

"And then?" she asked, clearly skeptical.

"Then, if we agree on the first step, we move on to the next."

She seemed surprised or unsettled that he had agreed to consider her plan. The way he saw it, there weren't a lot of options just now. He would deal with the official side of this mess as soon as Grace and Liam were someplace safe, and he knew just the place.

"Okay." She took a big breath. "Where do you have in mind?"

"I have a place kind of off the grid. It's isolated and difficult to find."

She nodded. "Sounds good. I have a bag with some extra cash and new IDs. Everything we need to…"

As if she'd realized that it sounded exactly like she planned to disappear, her voice trailed off.

"I get it." He shrugged. "You're prepared to run if necessary. You will gladly give up everything to keep Liam safe."

She squeezed her eyes shut for a moment before meeting his gaze once more. "I would. Including my life."

"That's not going to happen," he shot back. "I will not let that happen."

She took a deep breath. "Thank you."

His cell vibrated on his utility belt. He checked the screen. *Reynolds*. "I have to take this."

"I should check on Liam."

He gave her a nod as he accepted the call. "Hey, Reynolds, what's up?"

"Damn, boss, we've got ourselves a body," he said, his voice humming with excitement. "That's what's up. You should get over here to the Cashion place. This is bad. Really bad."

A new line of tension threaded through Rob. "A homicide?"

"Definitely. This guy has been stabbed like a couple dozen times. There's blood everywhere."

Well, hell. "Okay, stay out of the blood. Don't touch anything and see if we can get Snelling over there."

"Will do."

Sergeant David Snelling was top-notch. He led an excellent team of forensic analysts.

"I'll be there in five."

The Cashion place was only a couple of miles away. Rob couldn't help thinking of the intruder who'd been sleeping in the garage at the Sells home. The Cashion home was only blocks from there. He made a call to Deputy Lyle Carter to get him over to the inn. He was close by already and would arrive in the next couple of minutes. Then he went in search of Grace. He found her talking with Diane.

To Grace he said, "There's something I need to check on, but I'll be right back. Deputy Carter will be here, right outside, if you need anything before I'm back. Do not go anywhere without me."

"I'll be here," Grace assured him.

"Now, that sounds intriguing," Diane said with a wink in Rob's direction.

He only smiled and gave the two a nod. "Ladies." On second thought, he added, "And Liam."

Liam was too busy shoving cookies into his mouth to do anything but grin.

Rob pulled on his cap as he headed for his SUV. After Carter arrived, he gave the deputy his instructions before loading up. The drive to the Cashion home took less than five minutes.

If Snelling was not already tied up with another scene, it would take him maybe half an hour to arrive. The second cruiser on-site told Rob that Reynolds had called in Donnie Prater. The youngest and newest of the deputies assigned to this substation was already knocking on the doors of neighbors. Reynolds was rolling out the crime scene tape around the Cashions' detached garage.

Rob pulled to the side of the street and climbed out of his vehicle. He walked to the garage, where the overhead door remained closed. The walk-through door on the side stood open. No sign of the home-owners. Danny Cashion was a lifelong Mountain resident. His wife, Tasha, was a transplant from Knoxville. The couple's two sons were in college.

Reynolds waited for Rob to get close enough to talk in lowered voices.

"Snelling is on his way. The Cashions are in the house. I've interviewed them already. They were on a mini vacation for the weekend and just got back to find…this."

"Let's have a look." They didn't get homicides around here very often. Not the way they did down-town. The lack of violence and trouble overall was one of the reasons most residents had chosen the Moun-tain.

The family's minivan was parked in the garage, but it was a double-car garage and a good-sized one at that, so moving around the vehicle was no prob-lem. The victim lay on the floor in the vacant bay. Like Reynolds had said, he'd been stabbed repeat-edly. Probably a dozen or more times.

"This guy must have really pissed someone off."

"Looks that way," Reynolds agreed. "The ME is on his way."

"Did you find any ID?"

"That's the really weird part," Reynolds said as he pulled out his phone. "This guy is from California."

A warning sounded in Rob's brain. He instantly noted the guy's blond hair and sightless pale blue eyes staring at the ceiling. He judged the victim to be midthirties. Oh, damn.

Reynolds showed him the image of a driver's license on his phone. "Adam Locke. He was just released from—"

"Did you run his license?" Something cold and dark stirred in Rob's gut. Of course he had. It was straight out of the training manual.

"I did. Got a hit ASAP. A Detective Lance Gibbons called me, like, instantly. Said he's getting on a plane right now and that he'd be here tonight."

As much as Rob hated that a homicide had occurred in his jurisdiction, this could potentially be a huge relief for Grace Myers. He took out his own cell and zoomed in on the victim's face. He snapped a pic. Then he pulled a pair of gloves from his coat pocket and crouched down. He checked the victim's finger, then an arm, to judge the path of rigor mortis. He'd been here a little while. He was in full rigor.

"Okay, as long as you have things under control here, I need to…" Rob pushed to his feet. How the hell did he explain what he had to do? "I have to finish up at the inn. As soon as you hear from Gibbons, let me know."

Rob felt bad about leaving Reynolds with this mess, but it was only until he had Grace settled at the cabin. Then he'd be back.

"Don't worry about me," Reynolds assured him with possibly a little too much bravado. "I've got this."

Rob had a last look at the dead guy before returning to his SUV. He struggled to drive slowly away from the new crime scene. He really wanted to believe this was a good thing. If this victim actually was Adam Locke, then Grace was free of him and the world was a safer place.

The trouble lay in who murdered him and the connection to Grace and her son.

Lookout Inn, 3:30 p.m.

GRACE TRIED TO focus on anything else for the half hour or so that Rob was gone, but she couldn't. Her mind kept going back to the last time she'd seen Adam. He'd insisted on talking to her. He'd promised the police that if they allowed him to see her he would confess to all his victims—even the ones they didn't know about.

Of course, he hadn't. After the meeting he'd only laughed and said he was innocent.

Fury rushed through her when she thought of how he'd used her, how he'd treated her like another of his puppets. She supposed she should be thankful that he hadn't killed her. In that short meeting Gibbons had pressured her into, Adam had insisted that he would never have hurt her. He'd claimed to be just as surprised by what she'd found in the basement as she was and that he'd chased her through those woods at her father's cabin to try to warn her that she might not be safe. Everything that had come out of his mouth was a lie.

He'd promised her they would be together again someday, and until then she was to take good care of his son.

His son. Not their son.

More of that fury boiled up inside her. How the hell had he found her? What did he expect to accomplish by coming here? She was never going to allow him anywhere near Liam. No judge in this country would ever give him any sort of visitation rights— even if he did somehow manage to escape charges for all that he had done.

But he wouldn't. She wouldn't allow him to escape justice.

She had found that woman in the basement. Alicia Holder had said a man with blond hair and blue eyes had put her there. To Grace's knowledge, no other prints were found beyond Adam's. He had claimed that the perpetrator had likely used gloves. Since Alicia—as well as all his other victims—was dead, she couldn't testify. Without the evidence in that basement room, all Gibbons had was Grace's account of how she had found the woman.

But then Grace had run away when she couldn't catch up with the woman. And why wouldn't she? She may have been in shock but she wasn't stupid. She had known that when Adam came home and discovered what she had done he would kill her. The same way he likely killed that poor woman. She'd been found in an alley. As it turned out, she'd been homeless. Many of his victims had been. Young women who'd made the mistake of deciding they would be happier on their own or who had drug issues and had been cast out by their families. Prostitutes. People society sometimes ignored. Each one was found wearing nothing but the heart-shaped locket with their photo inside wrapped around their cold, dead fingers. This was the one thing he always left behind. After endless torture, he'd stabbed each victim directly in the heart—as if he'd studied the organ and knew exactly how to slide the blade into precisely the right place. Then he stabbed them over and over as if he'd suddenly lost control.

There had been three in a two-year period. Then he'd stopped. Gibbons and his profiler had speculated that after Adam married Grace he'd stopped for a while. The woman in the basement was the only other known victim.

Grace supposed it was possible he had tried to stop, but as the pressure of fatherhood closed in on him, perhaps he broke and sought out the pleasure he got from taking a victim.

She rolled her eyes. She was not giving that bastard one iota of slack. He had brutalized and murdered at least four women. He didn't deserve to keep breathing, but he would. The best she could hope for was that he would spend the rest of his life in prison.

"You okay, Grace?"

Grace snapped back to the present and realized

Diane was right beside her. "Sorry. I was deep in the past."

"I should get started setting up the dining room," Diane suggested. "I'm not sure Liam will hold a bite of supper after eating all those cookies."

Somehow Grace managed a soft chuckle. "Well, a few extra cookies now and then won't hurt."

Diane grinned. "You should never say that around a yoga instructor."

Grace laughed outright this time. "Sorry. You're right. Bad mommy."

As if Liam realized they were talking about him, he rushed over to Diane and tugged at her apron. "I can take the *nackins.*"

"You can," Diane assured him. She handed him the basket that held the freshly laundered and folded cloth napkins. "Mom can do the silverware."

Grace gave her a salute. "Aye aye, captain."

As they worked to ready the table for their guests, Grace wasn't sure she could eat a thing either. The idea that her ex-husband was out there somewhere a free man wouldn't let go of her. She couldn't possibly eat.

Adam hadn't actually ever agreed to the divorce, but under the circumstances, Grace was able to push it through without his agreement. Would that change now that the murder charge against him might very well be dropped completely in the end?

God, she hadn't thought of that until just now.

She supposed it didn't matter. She would never be that woman again.

But it would matter if he mounted a legal battle.

The sound of the front door opening and then closing had Grace hurrying into the parlor. The weary look on Rob's face tightened the band around her chest. Had something more happened related to her situation?

Stop, Grace. She was overreacting. Rob had an entire community to worry about. She wasn't the only person with problems. Hers were just more twisted and complicated than most.

"We should talk privately."

Oh, dear God. It was about her situation. She nodded. "I'll let Diane know."

Grace hurried to the dining room. "Diane, do you mind seeing after Liam for a while? Deputy Vaughn is back and…"

Diane nodded. "Got it." She smiled at Liam. "Little man and I have dinner under control." She waved Grace off. "Shoo."

"Shoo, Mommy," Liam repeated with a giggle.

Grace managed a laugh and left them to it. Rob wasn't in the parlor anymore, so she walked quickly toward her private quarters and found him waiting there. This must be bad, she decided, to warrant this level of privacy.

She closed the door behind her and steeled herself.

"There was a murder just a couple of miles from here."

Her breath caught. A murder? "What happened?"

He moved toward her and she suddenly wished she hadn't asked. Wished she didn't need to know.

He withdrew his cell phone and tapped the screen. "Do you know this man?"

Grace stared at the image, a close-up of a face she knew as well as her own. Her brain froze up for a second. She blinked. Told herself to look again.

"It's him. It's Adam." Something hot rushed through her body, followed immediately by an icy cold. She swayed. Rob's hand reached out and steadied her.

"You're certain?" he prodded.

"Yes. It's him. What happened?" The question popped out all on its own, even though she really didn't care. Judging by the pallor of his skin, he appeared to be dead, and some part of her was jumping up and down and shouting that she was free. Free!

"Stabbed multiple times."

She stared at him, reminded herself to breathe. "Like his victims."

"Looks that way."

"How long…?" She drew in another desperate burst of air. "Do you have any idea when this happened?"

"The Cashions were away for the weekend. When they came home this afternoon, they found him, so we really can't be sure just yet. I'm guessing early this morning. Maybe the middle of the night. The medical examiner will give us more on time of death after he's had a chance to examine the victim. Obviously only hours after he was here."

Grace made her way to the closest chair and dropped into it. "I'm certain I should be feeling something, but I only feel numb."

Rob took a seat on the sofa directly across from her. "The emotions will come later when your mind has been able to absorb the reality of what's happened."

She understood this from before, but still… Adam was dead. She didn't have to worry about him coming after her. She could live her life any way she chose. She could—

A new question bobbed to the surface of the haze currently shrouding her. "Who killed him?"

"That's the problem." Rob turned the navy cap that matched his uniform around and around in his hands. "Like you said, he was stabbed in a manner consistent with that of his victims. No one here except you knew him—I'm assuming—so that can only mean one thing."

The reality of what he was saying slammed into her. Her heart dropped into her belly, and she wanted to rush into the kitchen and grab Liam. Hold him tight. "Someone followed him here…or came with him. One of his followers."

"It's the only logical explanation."

Adam had followers. Before his identity was even known, there were those who praised the work of the Sweetheart Killer. Like all criminals who rose to notoriety, there were fans. After his arrest, the fan letters had poured in. The fact that Adam had been a handsome man—a charismatic man—had garnered him a huge audience.

The fans had flocked to the home she and Adam had shared. The place had to be guarded to prevent them from going inside. His office in the business district and her father's cabin in Lake Tahoe had both become shrines to Adam Locke.

Well before that, Grace and baby Liam had gone into hiding.

"I have to leave." She rocketed to her feet. "I have to get Liam to safety." Adam was dead, but if one of his fanatical followers was here, they wouldn't be safe. All manner of threats had been made against her two years ago by those obsessed with Adam Locke.

"Grace," he said softly, too softly, "I know I promised you that I'd help you do that, but this has changed everything."

"How?" She shook her head. "I don't understand. We could be in danger. We can't stay here."

"Detective Gibbons is on his way."

If he'd wielded a physical blow, he could not have shaken her more violently. "What does his coming have to do with me?" That fluctuation between hot and cold started again. She couldn't stop it.

"We have to do this the right way. Locke came here after you. Gibbons will want to talk to you. He'll want to go over what happened on Sunday evening."

"None of this…" Fury tightened her lips. "Not his murder… Nothing is more important than my son's safety. I don't care what Gibbons wants."

"If you take off before this is finished, then Locke will still be haunting you, because you'll look guilty. If you hold on just long enough to get through this, then you can put it behind you once and for all."

He was right. She recognized he was, but that didn't make her like it one little bit.

"I just need to be sure my son is protected."

"I'm going to ensure that the two deputies on shift tonight drive by every hour or so, and I'm checking into the inn and staying right here on this sofa."

"You…" She searched his face. "You would do that for us?"

"I will do whatever it takes to keep the two of you safe. You have my word on that."

"Thank you." She blinked to hold back the burn of tears. "There hasn't been anyone since my father died. It's just been Liam and me."

"That's not the case anymore, Grace. You have me and a whole community of people who admire and respect you. You are not alone."

She wanted desperately to cling to that hope, but what this man didn't understand just yet was that although Adam Locke was dead, his followers were not. By the time they finished or were caught, this whole community would rue the day Grace Myers arrived in their midst.

Chapter Six

Grace could only imagine the lengths to which Detective Lance Gibbons had gone to find a flight leaving San Francisco for Chattanooga as soon as he heard the news. The strings he must have pulled to get on that flight. The minute he had landed, he'd gone straight to the morgue to view the body. Now he was headed here. Based on the call Rob had received from the man, Gibbons should be here in the next fifteen minutes.

The memory of the way he had hammered her for answers during those first few days in the hospital after having Liam assailed her. He'd been ruthless, pushing her as if she were the criminal. The manhunt for Adam had been ongoing with no results. No one had called in to say they had seen him. Not even the usual crazies. It was as if Adam had put out the word for radio silence and the world had obeyed.

But Gibbons had had a plan even then. Like Grace, he had known that Adam would want to see his son. She had begged for police protection in the hospital, but Gibbons had put a single guard on her room and left it at that. Her father had remained at her side until his heart attack. She hadn't even been able to make his funeral arrangements for days after his death because she was still in the hospital. The doctor kept saying she couldn't be released just yet.

Later Grace had learned that Gibbons had seen to it that she stayed in the hospital three extra days. His long shot had paid off. Two days after her father's death, Adam had stolen a doctor's ID badge and scrubs and entered the hospital. Gibbons had been waiting.

The pressure lowered on Grace for a while after that. She'd been able to leave the hospital and prepare for her father's funeral. It was at his graveside service that she'd learned about Adam's followers. A trio had shown up and attempted to abduct Liam. The two policemen assigned to watch her had done the best they could to hold them off. The funeral director had managed to get her and Liam away from the cemetery. A similar attack had occurred days later as she was leaving the pediatrician's office. That was when she had known she had to disappear.

Disturbed by the memories, she went to the bedroom to check on Liam. He had fallen asleep a little later than usual since Rob was here. The fact that Diane had stayed so late and Cara had returned had unsettled him. He was accustomed to there being only the two of them and the guests after eight in the evening. Generally, they only saw the guests passing through the lobby on the way to their rooms after dinner or an evening out.

Tonight everyone had rallied around Grace. Even the Wilborns had returned for a short time to see if their help was needed. Both Cara and Diane had been stunned by her story and promised to do whatever was necessary to help her keep Liam safe.

Grace sat down on the bedside now and swiped the hair from her sweet child's eyes. Would they feel the same way if someone they knew and cared about lost their lives to one of her ex-husband's followers?

She hoped that did not happen. Enough lives had been lost to Adam Locke's evil deeds, but there was no way to know when the other shoe would drop. If a follower had for whatever reason murdered Adam, she or he was likely far more deranged than the average fan. It was possible Adam had rebuked him or her for some reason. Or perhaps the killer wanted to prove he or she was better.

At the soft knock Grace opened the parlor door expecting to find Rob, but it was Cara and Diane.

First one and then the other hugged Grace tightly. "That detective from San Fran is here," Diane explained.

"We can stay with Liam if you'd like to see him," Cara offered. "He says he doesn't need to interview either of us just yet."

Diane made a face. "I don't like him."

The two women could not be more different. With dark spiky hair and dark eyes, Diane was thin but well toned thanks to her dedication to yoga. Every one of her fifty years showed in the lines on her face, but she didn't care. Never wore makeup. What you saw was what you got. Cara was more reserved. Her long blond hair was silky smooth, and she took great care with her makeup and dress. Though thin like Diane, she was more into running than yoga. Both were good friends to Grace. Better friends than she'd ever had in her adult life.

"I don't like him much either," she admitted.

"He wants to speak with you if you're ready," Cara said.

Grace would never be ready, but she had no choice. "Thank you."

Diane urged, "We will get through this."

"I really appreciate the two of you being here." Grace looked from one to the other and then did what she understood she must. She walked out, closed the door to their private quarters behind her and went to the kitchen. Since additional security was needed in light of the murder, Rob had ensured the new police presence was not overwhelming. Both deputies on duty for the night were dressed in plain clothes. Rob had spoken to the inn's two guests and explained the situation. Both had been far calmer about the situation than Grace had expected, and she greatly appreciated their understanding. This was not the sort of thing she wanted to see in a Yelp review.

For support, her gaze locked on Rob as she entered the kitchen. In her peripheral vision she noted that Gibbons stood at the island, his back to her. Grace walked wide around his position and straight to Rob's side. With heavy reluctance she faced the man who had added to her nightmares for weeks after finding that woman in the basement.

"Gia," Gibbons said with a nod.

"It's Grace," she corrected him. He certainly knew that by now, but he no doubt wanted to show he knew her for who she really was.

"Grace," he amended.

Though it had been just over two years since she had seen this man, he looked at least a decade older. She hadn't fared much better, she supposed. The sort of evil she had survived tended to age a person. Gibbons's suit was travel rumpled, and an evening shadow had darkened his jaw. His bloodshot eyes told her he still didn't sleep well. During the investigation, he'd told her he hadn't had a good night's sleep since earning his detective's shield. He was a homicide detective in a major city. The Locke case was just one of many nightmare cases he'd investigated. A good night's sleep likely wasn't a perk of the job for any investigator.

Gibbons was a good man. A husband, a father. Grace had wanted to like him, but she'd experienced firsthand the ugly side of his need to get the job done at all costs. It was not pleasant, even though her only crime had been falling in love with the wrong man. Add to that the need to protect her child, and she was basically a hostile witness, in the detective's opinion.

"Detective Gibbons and I have discussed how this is going to go," Rob said. "He has assured me you don't need an attorney present." Rob eyed the man with open suspicion. "But I don't know that I agree."

She had a feeling their earlier conversation hadn't gone as Rob expected. She wasn't surprised. Gibbons never bothered to hide his opinion that Grace hadn't told him everything. But she had. She had told him all that she knew about Adam. How they'd met...all of it.

"Why would I need an attorney?" She looked from Rob to Gibbons. Though she asked the question, the answer was simple. The victim was a serial killer. Her ex-husband. The father of her child. The one she had turned over to the police. Of course she was a suspect.

It didn't matter that Rob would insist this wasn't the case. She had been down this road before. Everyone knew when a person was murdered the spouse or ex-spouse was the primary suspect. She had more reason than the average ex to want Adam Locke dead. Last time around she had been a person of interest as well. No one had believed that she could live in a house where a victim was imprisoned and not know it was happening. But she hadn't. Adam had kept his victims bound and gagged as well as drugged. He'd expected to be finishing off his latest victim that day when he got the unexpected call from work. He'd anticipated being back before her last dose of sedative wore off. Except it hadn't worked out the way he'd anticipated.

Apparently, his journey here to find her hadn't either.

That was the only upside in all this. She was so damned glad he was dead. It was as if a steel cage had been removed from around her...except a glimmer of danger still lingered close by. It was impossible to fully understand the threat until the person who killed Adam was found.

"I'm certain you don't need an attorney," Gibbons said, drawing her back to the moment. "It is your right, however."

"Let's move on," Grace suggested. It was late, and she had no desire to drag this out any longer than necessary. "I would ask you to sit down, but I'm hoping this won't take that long."

"You've been here for two years," he said. "The deputy confirmed as much. On the plane I googled the inn and you, but oddly I found no photos of you or your son."

"I've been careful about that." She was only too happy for photos of the inn to be snapped but never with her or Liam in the frame. Even when she'd been given awards by the community leaders, she had been careful not to be in a photo.

She had learned the hard way that the internet was forever.

"Where were you before coming here?" Gibbons asked.

"If you want to know if Adam's been in contact with me, just ask." She refused to go into detail about where she was before finding this inn and starting her new life. "Where I've been is irrelevant to your investigation, I believe."

"I agree," Rob said. "The murder occurred here. I can't see how where she was prior to two years ago would have any bearing on the murder."

Grace pressed her lips together to hold back a smile. It was really nice to have someone on her side this time. Last time her father had just died, and all the people she'd thought were friends were suddenly gone. Busy. Unavailable. Not that she blamed a single one of them.

Bottom line, she had been on her own.

"Was he in contact with you at any time since you left California?" Gibbons asked. He watched her carefully over the top of his glasses as he waited for her to respond.

The glasses were new. She didn't recall seeing him with glasses last time. Looking at him more closely now, she noticed the light scattering of gray in his hair and in the stubble on his jaw.

"No. I was very careful. No one from my old life had any idea where I was or where I was going. After my father's death, there was nothing left in California for me."

"You had no reason to believe he was aware of your whereabouts now?"

"None at all." She thought of the visit to her porch. She felt confident Rob had already told him about this. "The first inkling I had that he might be in the area was when my son discovered a man walking around the house the other night. The man came onto the porch and looked into the window. I had no idea who he was, but my son said he had blue eyes. I have to admit that rattled me. But I assumed Adam was still in jail. It wasn't until the next day that I googled him and learned he'd been released."

"I would have warned you," Gibbons said, "had I known how to reach you."

Anger stirred deep in her belly. "You're well aware why you didn't know my location."

He glared at her, his own anger making an appearance. "We did what we thought was right."

"I'm sure you did," Grace replied. "But you did so with no care about the cost to me and my child."

"He was already on to us," Gibbons argued. "When we reached his office, he was gone—as you well know. Obviously he'd gotten a heads-up somehow."

On some level she understood that the police—Gibbons in particular—had thought that perhaps she had gotten cold feet and warned her husband they were coming. But that could not be farther from the truth. "He was on vacation. The call into work was an emergency. Did it not occur to you that he might return home before the end of his usual workday?" She shook her head. "Whatever you were thinking, rather than warn me that he was on the run or come to where I was—which was the most likely place he would go—you went into the house without a proper warrant."

"We had exigent circumstances since we believed you might be in danger," he argued. "Or that there could be a victim hidden in another secret room of the house."

Grace laughed. "Except I wasn't there and you knew I wasn't there. As for another victim, I never said there was another one." Thinking about the risk he took with her life and her son's infuriated her even now.

He shrugged. "We couldn't be sure of anything—not even your statement."

"Let's get this over with," she suggested. "Do your interview and then do your job. My son's life is at stake, and just like last time, I'm not going to stand around here and wait for you to provide the protection he needs."

Gibbons stared at the floor a moment before lifting his gaze back to hers. "We did what we thought was right."

"You said that already," she reminded him.

"I won't let you down this time, Gi—Grace," he promised.

"I'll be taking care of Grace and Liam's security," Rob countered.

Grace would never be able to thank this man enough.

"I do not want her leaving this property," Gibbons warned. "We lost track of her last time, and I don't want that to happen again until we finish this."

"No promises," Rob argued. "This could take weeks or months to sort out on your end. We will do whatever is best for our citizens on this end."

For the first time since she was a kid growing up in the woods well beyond the tourist setting of Lake Tahoe, Grace felt as if she belonged. She would never be able to thank Rob enough.

"The medical examiner provided me with a preliminary time of death," Gibbons was saying. "Between midnight and six this morning."

That would mean he'd been murdered only six to

twelve hours *after* coming here and looking at Liam through the window. Her heart shuddered. Had someone been with him or following him even then? She shuddered at the idea.

"He'll be able to pinpoint the time more closely as soon as he's completed the autopsy," Rob added.

Gibbons nodded. "I'm familiar with the routine." He shifted his attention to Grace. "Can you verify where you were during that time frame?"

She had expected the question. "I was here. Asleep with my son until about five and then I got up and started baking. My chef can confirm that I was in the kitchen elbow deep in dough when she arrived at five thirty."

No matter that she understood his questions were necessary, it still angered her that she was considered a suspect. Not that she hadn't dreamed of killing the bastard. It was the only way her son would ever be free. But she couldn't risk him losing his mother. She was no murderer, and the odds that she wouldn't get caught were not in her favor.

"Can anyone confirm you were here prior to Ms. Franks's arrival?"

She thought about that for a moment. There hadn't been any guests and Liam had been asleep. "No. I suppose not."

"Actually," Rob said, "I can vouch for her. A deputy was stationed outside the inn until Diane Franks arrived. Grace never left."

Grace stared up at him in a kind of shock. Why would he cover for her? He had to know Gibbons would attempt to confirm his statement. Whatever the case, she appreciated the effort.

"You had eyes on her vehicle all night?"

"Her SUV was in the garage and it never left."

"But she could have walked. It's less than two miles to the Cashion residence, where the murder occurred."

Now he was reaching.

"I would not have left my son alone," she argued.

"It was snowing," Rob stated. "And it was about twenty degrees. So no, that's not feasible."

"But you suspected Adam was here," Gibbons countered, his point directed at her. "How could you sleep knowing it was possible?"

"I couldn't be certain." This was not entirely true. She had found the necklace. She'd known that at the very least one of his followers was close by.

She should have given the damned locket to Rob... She shouldn't have pretended it didn't matter. Now if she told Gibbons about it, Rob would see it as her having hidden a perhaps important piece of evidence from him.

She really, really had to get her head on straight here.

Cutting herself some slack, she had sort of talked herself into believing it could be someone else. She'd come up with all sorts of other scenarios. The truth was, she hadn't been sure until she'd done that Google search the next day. "You can check my computer. Why would I have looked for information about him online if I'd known he was here and I had already killed him?"

"I suppose you wouldn't have," Gibbons admitted, "unless you'd done it to strengthen your alibi."

"Enough," Rob warned.

Grace jumped at his tone. Though he'd startled her, she was grateful he'd intervened.

"You are here—in my jurisdiction—and this is getting us nowhere," Rob warned him. "Unless you plan to carry out some sort of constructive investigation, then you should be on your way and allow us to do our jobs."

Gibbons held his glare with one of his own for a beat or two. Then his eyes pierced Grace. "He came here for a reason," he charged. "He wanted you back or he wanted his son and you dead. Whatever it was, if he brought help along, for some reason that helper turned on him. We need to know why that happened."

"I'm glad he's dead," Grace confessed. "I'm not going to lie. But I didn't kill him, and like you said, if he brought someone with him who did, then what's the motive? Does this other person want my son—his son—or just revenge for someone else?"

"So far," Rob pointed out, "you've talked about Locke having maybe brought a follower or a friend with him. Maybe this was a family member of one of his victims who's been posing as a follower, waiting for the right opportunity to take his revenge. Or one who learned of his impending release and then followed him here. He or she may be long gone now that the job is done."

Grace hadn't considered that option, but Rob was right. It was possible.

"We need to find whatever vehicle they were using," Gibbons suggested. "We started trying to track Locke as soon as he was released. He vanished before we could come up with other charges against him—at least to hold him until the original investigation was reopened. He didn't use public transportation, which would mean he likely drove or the person with him drove."

"So we're looking for a new arrival in town," Rob said. "One who came from the West Coast."

Grace thought of the two guests currently registered right here at the inn. One from California, the other from Seattle.

Rob's gaze collided with hers. "We're going to need to wake up your guests."

That was the last thing she wanted to do. Involving her guests was the worst possible scenario, but Rob was right—they fit the profile, so to speak. "I'll talk to them," Grace said. "In the morning. I will not disturb them tonight."

"I can't risk one or both disappearing when the police presence here tonight is gone," Gibbons countered.

"The police presence isn't going anywhere," Rob assured him. "I and one of my deputies will be here all night."

Gibbons straightened. "Well, I suppose under the circumstances I'll need to take a room as well. I'm not booked anywhere else." He turned to Grace. "I would think the multijurisdictional police presence would give you comfort."

How could she debate the statement? Gibbons knew Adam Locke better than anyone—maybe better than Grace.

Though she didn't find his presence here the least bit comforting, if his being on hand was in any way helpful in keeping Liam safe, she could deal with it.

Her son's safety was all that mattered.

"All right. Follow me and I'll get you registered."

He followed her to the registration desk, where she selected a key to one of the cabins. She could tolerate his presence but some distance was necessary.

"You're in cabin 15." She placed the key on the counter. "I'll fill in the necessary information. Your stay will be on the house. We appreciate all that law enforcement does to keep the community safe."

He picked up the key, his gaze searching hers for a moment. "Very well."

"I'll show you the way to the cabins," Rob suggested, saving Grace the trouble.

She'd have to remember to thank him later.

"I'll see you in the morning, Grace," Gibbons said before turning away.

She would see him. Only because she had no other choice.

Chapter Seven

It was well past midnight when Grace returned to her room. She found Diane and Cara pacing the floor. She peeked in on Liam, who remained fast asleep. Grace closed the door quietly and joined the others in her small parlor.

Rob had said he would check in with her once he'd walked the perimeter of the property and updated Reynolds. Grace felt immensely better with those two close by. She couldn't name what she felt with Gibbons in one of her cabins. She felt...uneasy. Restless. Like she needed to run as far and as fast as she could.

Stay calm. Focus on the necessary steps.

"This is insane," Diane insisted. "This guy cannot believe you killed that—that—"

"Monster," Cara said. She settled on the sofa and pulled her knees to her chest. "You saw the things we found on the internet," she said to Diane. Her attention shifted to Grace then. "I don't know how you survived."

Flashes of scrambling through the snow with him right behind her zoomed through her brain.

"I was lucky."

"You're also strong," Diane said. "Only someone with incredible courage could have gone through what you did and still be standing." She dropped into a chair. "My God, look at what you've accomplished here. You've built a great new life for you and Liam. It's amazing what you've done."

"Thank you." Grace dredged up a smile. "I'll just be thankful if we get through this and then move on with the rest of our lives."

She had to keep reminding herself that Adam was dead. It didn't feel real. No one was more grateful than her that he was gone, but it hadn't completely sunk in yet. She kept asking herself how she would deal with him, only to abruptly remember that she never had to deal with him again.

He was dead. Done. Gone. He was never coming back.

Except he'd likely brought someone with him, and that person could still be here. That person could be watching from a distance at this very moment.

She had an obligation to warn her employees. Just one more nightmare to add to the mix.

"There's a strong possibility he didn't come here alone."

"I read about him having followers," Cara said. "Does the detective from San Francisco feel someone like that may have come with him?"

"He does. Worse, there's a strong possibility that person may be a killer as well. May have killed Adam." At least, that was how Grace felt. "Until we know more, it's really important that both of you be very careful. I'll be having this same conversation with Paula and Karl."

"What about the guests?" Diane asked. "Are they in danger?"

Grace felt sick with the burden of this unholy mess. "The best way to look at this is that anyone close to me could be in danger."

Cara's eyes went wide. "Oh, no. Liam." She shook her head, her face a study in worry. "You should let me take him to my grandmother's cabin. We'd be safe there. Trust me, no one would ever find that cabin."

The offer gave Grace pause. "You know, I might have to take you up on that."

"The kid certainly adores Cara," Diane pointed out. "It could work."

The thought of not having Liam close was nearly more than Grace could bear. They had never been apart. Never separated by anything other than a wall. But this time there might not be a choice. His safety had to be her absolute top priority. No matter how painful to her mothering instincts.

Grace looked from one woman to the other. "Thank you. Both of you. I am so glad to have you in my life. Liam and I would be lost right now without you."

"I'm just sorry you didn't feel you could share this with us before," Cara said, the sadness in her tone tugging at Grace.

"You really can trust us," Diane chimed in.

"I know and I'm sorry," Grace confessed. "I thought I was doing the right thing."

"Anyway," Diane said with a shake of her head, "we're here and so is Rob. The man obviously has a serious crush on you."

Grace laughed off the suggestion. "He's a very nice man but—"

"Don't even go there," Cara interrupted. "The guy likes you and you should give him a chance. A little time for just the two of you would be a good thing. All the more reason to let me take Liam to the cabin."

"You could be right," Grace acknowledged. "And I promise to keep your offer in mind."

A soft rap at the door had Grace's heart rising into her throat. Rob opened the door and stepped in. "Ladies, if you're ready to go home, Deputy Reynolds will follow you and make sure you get inside safely. You live the nearest, Diane, so they'll go to your place first."

She hopped up. "Sounds good." She flashed Rob a big smile. "I always appreciate a man showing his gentlemanly side."

"I second that," Cara said as she joined Diane.

Grace hugged one and then the other. "See you in the morning."

Rob said, "I'll be back in a bit."

Had he and Detective Gibbons discussed the situation in greater detail? She hoped Gibbons was being entirely straight with them. If he was holding anything back, it could put Liam in danger. She really hoped he understood and cared about their safety.

She glanced at the clock. It was really late. She was exhausted. But obviously Rob wanted to talk, so she busied herself picking up Liam's toys and tidying the room. The idea of getting up at five to bake the day's sweets suddenly held no appeal.

Resentment tightened in her throat. How dare that monster come here and damage the carefully constructed life she and Liam had built. This was their home and they were happy here. It was the only place Liam remembered as home. She did not want anything to take that away from him. From her.

Another tap on the door and Rob was back.

She resisted the urge to sigh. She was so tired. "Can I get you anything, Rob? More coffee? A sandwich?" It wasn't until then that she realized they hadn't bothered with dinner. Diane had seen that the guests and Liam were taken care of, but Grace and Rob hadn't stopped long enough to think about food, much less to eat. "I just realized you worked through dinner."

"I'm fine. Thanks." He closed the door behind him. "Let's go over the situation with Gibbons without him around. That okay?"

"Sure. Although you might not want to hear my thoughts on the man."

Rob smiled, the expression a little dim considering he had to be as exhausted as she was. "I'm certain you've given him every benefit of the doubt."

Grace sat down on the sofa. She was too tired to keep standing. Rob had apparently been waiting for her cue, because he sat down in the chair facing her.

"Before," she said, thinking back though she would rather walk over hot coals than do so, "I was naive.

I'd never been involved with any sort of trouble and certainly not with a criminal." Twenty-nine seemed so far away, although she was only thirty-two now. It felt like a lifetime ago. "I had no idea how to handle the situation. On top of that, I had pregnancy brain— it was focused on other things rather than what my husband was up to."

"I can only imagine," he offered, "how frightening the whole situation was."

"It was surreal." She thought about the word. "It didn't feel real at the time. It was as if it were happening to someone else and I was only watching."

"You don't recall any friends or colleagues he had who might have been involved with what he was doing? No one he had the occasional beer with? Took a fishing trip with or whatever California guys do?"

She had to laugh at the last. "No. No one. But keep in mind that we started dating and less than a year later we were married and I was expecting a baby any second. We went straight from an accidental date to being parents."

"Accidental date?"

"I was supposed to have dinner with my first ever dating-app guy, but he didn't show. Adam's client had gotten ill and had to leave the restaurant before their food even arrived. He'd noticed me and saw that I was leaving before placing an order and figured things out. He suggested I have dinner with him if I wasn't opposed to salmon. We hit it off instantly. He was an executive at an advertising firm, and I did website work for clients. We shared a lot of the same interests and…" Her throat felt suddenly dry. "Then I made the mistake of my life."

Except she shouldn't say that since she wouldn't have Liam if not for having met Adam Locke.

"But there was no one he ever mentioned as a friend?"

"Sorry. No. He spent all his time talking about us and the baby. Occasionally he'd mention his work. But nothing about family. He'd said they were all dead and he didn't like talking about them."

"I'm confident Gibbons looked into the possibility of family."

"He did. He didn't take my word for anything, and I suppose he shouldn't have. My judgment was not what it should've been, obviously."

The memory of forgetting where she'd left Liam… of frantically searching for him…poked through the exhaustion. She blinked the memory away. The breakdown wasn't because something had been wrong with her. It was about her mind not being able to handle any more. Postpartum depression wasn't rare. It happened. Pile on top of that learning her husband was a serial killer and the abrupt death of her father, and her breakdown hadn't been surprising at all. Her mind had simply done what was necessary to preserve her sanity.

But this was an aspect of the past she would never share with anyone. Especially not with this man—a man she had started to think she might be able to develop feelings for. Who was she kidding? She already had. Frankly, she'd never expected to have those feelings for anyone again. This was a good thing. Really. It meant she was moving fully back toward normal.

Given her current circumstances, she wasn't so sure it was the right move. Her life was too damaged. Her past too haunted.

"Are you okay with having Gibbons here? He doesn't have to stay here. There are other places on the Mountain."

"No, it's okay. I suppose I should be grateful for his presence. I certainly am glad you and Deputy Reynolds are here." She made a face. "I am really sorry for all the trouble, Rob. This is a nightmare for you and your deputies."

"No trouble," he assured her. "A lady over on Bluebird Trail discovered someone had been sleeping in her garage. Then, after finding the body in the Cashion garage, I thought maybe it might have been Locke. But I'm wondering now if that's right considering he obviously had a vehicle of some sort. Why stay in some lady's garage? Is that the kind of thing he would do based on what you know about him?"

Grace thought about the question for a moment. Adam had always had a plan. Had always been a smooth operator. "I can't imagine him not having a plan—even a backup plan in place. He was very good at juggling things at work. He used to tell me how he kept management impressed. Since his employer and colleagues seemed as stunned by who he really was as anyone else, I suppose it was true. If you're asking me if I can see him staying in a garage…" She shrugged. "Maybe. If he was desperate enough. Otherwise, no. But whoever came with him or followed him may have much lower standards."

"Since he was released and could come and go as he pleased," Rob said, "I'm not feeling the idea that he'd take up residence in a garage. The Cashion place maybe. They were out of town. He may have picked an empty house at random. Noticed the pile of mail in the box and decided they were away. The place is close enough to have easy access to the inn."

A new thread of tension slid through her. "But if he was free to do as he pleased, why didn't he confront me face-to-face? Just walk through the door during business hours and make his presence known?"

This was the first time she'd considered the idea.

"And why hasn't Gibbons asked that question?" Rob added, considering the idea.

Grace felt the air escape her lungs. "Because he had a plan and no one was supposed to know." Her gaze latched on to Rob's. "Except he wanted me to know he was coming. That's why he came to the window and left that photo in my mailbox. He wanted me to be afraid. Gibbons probably suspects as much. He's well versed in the MO. There were always indications that the Sweetheart Killer selected his victims in advance. They were never random, although his selection pool was—mostly homeless people. Runaways. Women working the streets. Those who knew the victims would talk about gifts they had received just days before going missing. Chocolates. Flowers. The sort of things a man gives a woman when he's trying to woo her."

The doorbell rang and Grace jumped. At night, when she locked up, the only way to access the inn was to have a key or to ring the bell, which sounded only in her private quarters.

By the time she was on her feet, Rob was already across the room. "You expecting anyone?"

"No. Could it be Deputy Reynolds?" She followed him into the lobby.

"He'd call my cell."

Her heart was pounding by the time they reached the front entrance. Rob checked the security viewfinder. He frowned and turned to Grace. "Did you order pizza?"

"No. Maybe one of the guests. There are flyers from the local restaurants that deliver in all the rooms and cabins."

Rob opened the door. "Evening," he said to the delivery guy. "You have a name on that order?"

The deliveryman looked from Rob to Grace and back. "Grace Myers."

Grace shook her head. "I didn't order pizza."

The delivery guy dug out his cell phone. "Says here the call was made by Grace Myers." He rattled off the phone number.

The number was hers, but she hadn't called anyone.

"How much?" Rob asked.

"Twenty-eight fifty."

Rob paid the man and took the pizza. He closed the door and locked it. Then to Grace he said, "Check your cell."

She hurried back to her parlor, Rob right on her heels. She scanned the room for her phone. She couldn't remember when she'd had it last. Then she spotted it on the counter.

Scrolling through her recent calls, she saw there was only one she didn't recognize, and it wasn't one of her contacts. She pressed the number and waited through two rings.

"All Night Pizza."

"Sorry," she said and disconnected the call. Her gaze lifted to Rob's. "The call came from my phone."

She couldn't have made the call and forgotten. There had to be a mistake. Right? Or had she ordered pizza for Rob and Deputy Reynolds and forgotten?

"Maybe Diane or Cara placed the order and then forgot to tell you," Rob suggested.

"Maybe." In spite of everything, her appetite stirred with the scent of pizza filling the room. "Whatever the case, we shouldn't let good pizza go to waste." She produced a smile. "I could eat a slice."

He nodded. "Same here. I'll take some out to Reynolds too.

"I was thinking," he said while she rounded up plates and napkins, "I might park myself on the sofa in the lobby. The one by the fireplace. I'll have a direct view of the front entrance as well as your door."

She nodded. "Sure. Do you plan to spend more than just tonight? I'm happy to give you a room."

He didn't hesitate. "Yeah. I'd like to, as long as you don't have an issue with me being here."

"Absolutely not." She may have said that a little too quickly, but it was true. Particularly now that this unexplained delivery had arrived. "I'm glad you're here."

His smile made her heart feel just a little lighter. "Circumstances notwithstanding, I'm glad I'm here too."

She felt the urge to tell him about the breakdown and how every time something like this pizza delivery happened, she felt terrified that she was losing her grip again…but she wouldn't. It was bad enough he knew the deepest, darkest of her secrets. Having him know anything else negative was just too much. She really had expected to spend the rest of her life alone, except for her son. Since moving here and becoming so entrenched in the community, then becoming friends with Rob, she found herself thinking maybe she could let someone else in. Whenever the idea popped into her head, she dismissed it immediately because she was afraid to hope.

She would not feel that way now. No matter that her world had turned a little upside down in the past twenty-four hours, she refused to give up on a brighter future. She wanted a future with someone like Rob in it. No, not *like* Rob. With Rob himself, she amended.

Maybe that was wishful thinking, but there was no harm in wishing.

"Thank you, by the way," she offered, "for covering for me with Gibbons."

He shrugged. "It was true. Deputy Reynolds was

concerned about the call, so he hung around until Diane arrived."

Grace shook her head. "I had no idea, but I'm certainly grateful."

"Just part of the job," he insisted.

In Grace's opinion, it was above and beyond.

"Tell me about your family, Rob." She bit into a slice of pizza and her taste buds screamed in delight. She was starving and hadn't realized it. "I know you have a brother in the military and a sister, but not much else."

Listening to stories about someone else's life would be a refreshing change.

"That's right. My younger brother is in the army, stationed in Colorado. My sister lives in Nashville. Her husband is a sound engineer at one of the labels there, and she's an interior designer to the celebrities. They're talking about starting a family. My mom is überexcited since she has no grandchildren yet. My father died a few years ago, and I think she's a little lonely. She lives in Chattanooga in the home where we grew up. She wants nothing more, she insists, than to have it filled with the laughter of grandchildren."

"You're the oldest?" Grace had gotten that idea somewhere.

"I am." He tore off a bite of pizza and hummed his appreciation. "This is good. Whoever ordered it, I'm glad they did."

Grace opted not to think about it. "Why aren't you married and having grandchildren for your mother?"

There, she'd done it. Asked the most personal of questions. Something she never ever did for fear of having the same asked of her. Then again, he knew most of her personal information.

He laughed. Swallowed. Then laughed again. "Actually, about a year ago I thought I was on my way. But my fiancée changed her mind. She married someone else, and now they're a few weeks away from having their first kid together."

"Oh, wow. That…" She wasn't sure what to say.

"Sucks?" he suggested.

"Yeah." Grace glanced around. "I should get us something to drink." She got up and went to the refrigerator. It was smaller than average, kitchenette size, but it worked. She opened the door and reached for a couple of bottles of water.

She stalled, her hand midreach. On the glass shelf was the big ring of the dozens of keys to the inn and its many locks. The metal keys were coated with moisture from sitting so long in the fridge.

Questions zoomed through her mind, and it literally hurt not to make a sound of surprise. Instead, she removed the keys and placed them on the counter, careful that Rob didn't notice. Then she grabbed the bottles of water and elbowed the door closed.

Everything was fine. She was fine.

This had just been a crazy day. Liam may have put the keys in the fridge. Cara or Diane may have ordered the pizza and forgotten.

None of this meant she was losing her grip again. She was fine. Everything was fine.

The man who'd destroyed her life and pushed her father into an early grave was dead.

How could it not be fine?

Chapter Eight

Tuesday, February 20, 6:00 a.m.

Grace washed her hands thoroughly. The baking hadn't provided the mindless relaxation it usually did. There were a couple of reasons for that, she admitted as she reached for a towel.

One, she'd come into the kitchen at five to get started and her favorite rolling pin had been in the oven. It was a miracle she spotted it as she turned on the oven to preheat. She considered the possibility that Liam had tucked it into the oven as he had the keys in the fridge in their little kitchenette. But she couldn't be sure he'd done either. She planned to ask him when he was up.

But did she really want to know?

Wasn't it easier just to assume...to pretend?

The alternative was the very real possibility she was on her way to a new breakdown. She'd certainly been there before. Grace pressed her fingers to her lips to stop their trembling. Maybe she was just growing more absent-minded. Or perhaps all the fear and drama of the past twenty-four hours had triggered that anxiety she kept hidden so carefully. Anxiety could lead to other issues. No one knew better than her.

It would be so easy to pretend the anxiety and panic that too often crept its way in didn't exist, which was what she generally did. The panic attacks and generalized anxiety had appeared after finding the woman in the basement and then having to run for her life, not to mention losing her father. The one doctor she had dared to discuss the situation with had explained that when the stress of life became too much, a person's mind could simply shut down completely or do so intermittently. It was a way to reduce the level of anxiety. Panic attacks were not unusual in a situation such as the one she had survived. She was only human, after all.

The symptoms were easy to recognize once you had been down that path. Rapid heart rate. Constant lingering fear that something terrible was about to happen and there was nothing you could do to stop it. Forgetfulness. Confusion.

The crash had come suddenly and with extreme ferocity that first time. Typical, the doctor had explained. Her mind and body hadn't known what to expect, so the reaction was magnified. Her father's longtime house manager had taken Grace in. Valentina Hicks, an old hippie who lived mostly off the grid near the community where Grace had grown up, had known all the right things to do. She claimed to have helped many of her flower-child friends through their breakdowns in the seventies. Whatever she was or had done, Val had kept Grace and Liam safe for months. Long enough for Grace to figure out a plan.

She'd been wrong before when she said there was no other family. Val was family, even if Grace hadn't seen her or spoken to her in more than two years. Val had insisted that Grace not look back when she left. No calls. No letters. Nothing that could leave a trail. During their stay with her, Val had taught her about taking care of herself when the burdens around her grew too large.

Sadly, with cops everywhere and a nearly three-year-old running around, not to mention an inn to manage, it wasn't like she could slip away for a couple of hours of meditation or a nice long run. At this point she doubted even that would work.

Adam Locke, the man who had devastated her life, was dead.

She'd lain in bed last night and tried to think of anyone she remembered being a friend to him when they were married. Anyone he'd ever mentioned. But there was no one. Not a single person she could recall in their twelve months together. Grace hadn't really spent a lot of time when they were together wondering about his lack of friends. They were young, in love and expecting a baby. Then, after all hell broke loose, she'd been too busy trying to survive and set up a whole new life for her and Liam. But now, the idea that someone had murdered Adam left her no choice. She forced herself to think.

Obviously the person could have been someone else he'd harmed. There were at least four victims left in his wake. Maybe a family member of one of those victims had been following his case and decided to see justice served on his or her own terms. Particularly after the abrupt release on a damned technicality.

If that were the case, she and Liam likely had nothing to fear from the person who had murdered Adam.

Unless—and this was the part that had taken root during the wee hours of this morning—this same person saw Liam as a future threat. Some would believe that being the son of a killer meant Liam would be a killer as well.

But that wasn't true. Liam was an innocent child who knew nothing of his evil father. If Grace had her way, he would never know anything about the man.

It was the only way she knew to protect him.

Was that the right thing to do? She had no idea. Babies didn't come with an instruction manual. Although there was plenty written about the best ways to raise a child, the truth was, most people learned by trial and error.

In any event, this was Grace's error to make. Liam would never hear about Adam Locke from her.

The timer sounded, and Grace shook off the worrisome thoughts. She went to the stove and shut off the timer, then removed the muffins from the oven. A batch of chocolate chip cookies was already cooling on the counter.

"Smells great in here," Rob said as he entered the kitchen. He surveyed the cookies on the counter. "You do this every morning?"

"I do." Grace dumped the muffins onto another cooling rack. She quickly placed them in a basket and covered them. She passed the basket to Rob. "Would you put that on the buffet next to the toaster?"

"Sure."

He accepted the basket and headed for the door.

"While you're at it, make yourself a plate. All guests of the inn get breakfast."

"You don't have to tell me twice," he said before pushing through the swinging door that separated the kitchen from the dining room.

Grace smiled, especially grateful for even the small things this morning. She removed her oven mitts and left the kitchen, using the door that led into the hall and heading for their private quarters. Once inside, she turned off the app on her phone and walked into the bedroom where Liam still slept. The baby monitor was the best invention since sliced bread, in her opinion. It allowed her to be in the kitchen while Liam still slept. Though she was only a few yards away, she preferred being able to hear and see him. The app she had downloaded onto her phone prevented the need for carrying around a second device. It was perfect for her needs.

"Good morning, little guy," she said to her sleeping child.

His eyes fluttered open, and her heart stumbled before she could clear away the memory of Adam's.

"I 'mell cookies." Liam grinned sleepily.

"You do, but first you need to have breakfast with Deputy Rob. He's already in the dining room."

Liam tossed off the covers. "Yay!"

Their morning routine went far more quickly since Liam couldn't wait to have breakfast with Rob. His affection for the man gave her a warm feeling. Whether there was ever to be more than friendship between her and Rob, she was grateful for his presence in her son's life.

She and Liam joined Rob in the dining room. Mr. Pierce and Mr. Brower were already seated, their plates loaded with Diane's fabulous breakfast offerings.

"Did you invite Deputy Reynolds in?" she asked Rob, remembering belatedly that he'd had outside surveillance duty last night.

"I sent him home around two this morning," Rob explained.

"Good." Grace was glad to hear the deputy hadn't spent a cold night in his vehicle.

"Any news on the *m-u-r-d-e-r*—" Henry Brower glanced at Liam and made a face "—that occurred not far from here?" he asked. His brow furrowed in concern. "I'm not complaining, but there's been a little more excitement than I expected."

"We're usually very quiet around here," Grace assured him, grateful he'd spelled out the word. Liam remained focused on his muffin. "Hopefully we've seen the last of the unusual excitement." She didn't like making promises she couldn't keep, but she certainly didn't want her guests thinking this sort of activity was the norm.

"The crime rate in the area is very low," Rob assured him. "We're about seventy-odd percent below the national average, but things do happen occasionally."

Brower nodded as he reached for his coffee. "That's certainly good to hear."

Grace smiled. "It is one of the reasons I chose the area and brought this inn back to life. It's a lovely community."

If Mr. Pierce had any thoughts on the activities since his arrival, he kept them to himself. Coming from LA, he would no doubt recall the Sweetheart Killer case. He couldn't possibly have missed it. As soon as the name of the victim was released, he would know that an infamous San Francisco serial killer had been murdered on the Mountain. Then he would notice the cops hanging around the inn, and before long he would put two and two together and he would recognize Grace.

There was no way to stop it.

Her appetite vanished and she thought of Cara's offer. Maybe Liam would be safer away from all this.

"Mr. Brower," Rob said, "your company is thinking of opening a division in Chattanooga?"

Grace looked from Rob to her guest. Evidently, Rob had done some research. She hoped his questions wouldn't upset the guests, but then again, it was necessary. As much as she despised the idea, it was the only way to ensure this nightmare ended without harm to Grace and her son—or anyone else, for that matter.

"We are," the older man said. "Chattanooga is

currently an up-and-comer. We thought long and hard about whether to go with Nashville or Chattanooga, and ultimately we believe we'll find a better home here versus in Music City."

"Nashville is a busy place," Rob agreed. "For now, it's easier to gain an identity in Chattanooga."

"Exactly our thoughts," Brower agreed. He studied Rob a moment. "You're the deputy in charge of this small community, isn't that right?"

Rob nodded. "I am."

Brower looked from Rob to Grace. "Should we be concerned that you're here at the inn in light of the other situation?"

Grace had hoped they were beyond that subject.

"You shouldn't be concerned at all." Rob flashed his trademark charming smile. "My reason for being at the inn is personal."

Grace felt her face flush. Their guests glanced at her, which didn't help, but she supposed this was a better option than the truth.

As if fate had decided to ramp up her already rising anxiety, Pierce stared a good deal longer at her. Just when Grace felt he might finally look away, he said, "Maybe you knew the *v-i-c-t-i-m*."

If he hadn't continued to stare at her, as if he were daring her to deny his suggestion, she might have considered his comment innocent. But the glimmer of certainty, of challenge, in his eyes told her he was dead serious and that he knew he was right.

"Well," Grace replied, opting to sidestep his obvious jab, "I'm certain that, whoever he was, Deputy

Vaughn will see that the investigation is conducted carefully and thoroughly."

"Count on it." Rob seconded her assertion.

To add fuel to the fire of her uneasiness, Detective Gibbons appeared, wearing the same rumpled suit and still in need of a shave.

Grace pushed back from the table. She picked up her son's plate. "Liam, let's see how things are going in the kitchen." He scooted out of his chair and followed her, nibbling on his muffin as he went.

She hurried through the swinging door while Gibbons was still poking around the coffee urn. She helped Liam onto a stool at the island and placed his plate in front of him.

"You f'got mine juice," her little boy said, staring up at her.

"I'll pour you some more." She went to the refrigerator and grabbed the orange juice.

Diane watched her. "You okay?" She kept her voice low.

Grace managed a nod. "The man from LA may have figured out…" She glanced at Liam. "Things."

"Maybe Cara's offer was the right thing," Diane said. She shook her head. "I'm all for standing your ground, but this may get hairy."

Unfortunately, her friend was right. Grace had to consider Liam's safety and well-being above all else.

ROB WAS NOT happy this Pierce guy had upset Grace. But he let it go for her sake. She would not want him going off on one of her guests.

"Morning," Gibbons said as he placed his coffee on the table. He turned back to the buffet and reached for a plate.

"Morning," Rob said.

Brower did the same.

Pierce seemed to still have that itch he couldn't ignore. He stared at Rob. "That's why you're hanging around, isn't it? Because she knew the murdered guy?"

Brower shot him a squeamish look.

Gibbons tossed the man a glance as well.

Rob decided there was no help for what he had to do. "Mr. Pierce, you're a guest in this inn, so I'm going to be as nice about this as I can. What you're referring to is an official police investigation. I am not going to discuss it with you, and neither is anyone else employed at the inn. If you're interested in headlines for that paper you work for, I'll give you one."

Joe Pierce's stare turned triumphant. "That would be helpful."

"Here goes," Rob said, pressing the other man with his gaze. "How does a freelance reporter from LA know to come to a remote Tennessee community just in time for an infamous serial killer's murder? That's an article I would read for sure."

"Me too." Gibbons plopped his plate on the table and eyed Pierce. "Why don't you explain how that happened?"

Pierce's glare was back. "And who the hell are you?"

"Detective Lance Gibbons, SFPD."

Pierce's attention shifted back to his half-eaten breakfast. "I had this reservation last week."

"All the more reason to wonder why," Gibbons said.

Rob picked up a slice of bacon and tore off a bite. Maybe he did like Gibbons after all.

When Pierce said nothing, Rob said, "We're all listening, Pierce."

"I have a friend," the reporter said, "who told me the warrant was under review before it was public knowledge."

Gibbons shrugged. "How did that lead you to making a reservation in Chattanooga, Tennessee? Not a logical leap under any circumstances I can fathom."

Except one, Rob understood. This guy had a source.

Pierce grinned. "I guess you've got me on that one. I got a note, delivered to my office. The note said the story was here. In the Chattanooga area at this inn. I had no idea what that meant until I arrived."

"How did you know to arrive when you did?" Rob asked. "There was no body at that point."

"I was told there would be big news here this week, and that if I was smart I'd be at this inn to hear it." He shrugged. "I wasn't taking any chances, so I came on Monday."

Brower stood. "I'm confident this discussion will get even more titillating, but I certainly have nothing to add."

Rob agreed with the guy's conclusion. "Have a nice day, Mr. Brower."

Brower gave him a nod and exited the dining room.

"Any ideas on who sent the note?" Gibbons demanded of the remaining guest.

Pierce shook his head. "And even if I did know, I wouldn't tell you."

Gibbons shrugged. "Nothing on the note that might prove useful to my investigation?"

"Our investigation," Rob pointed out.

Gibbons made a nod of acquiescence.

"Not a single thing. No name. No address. No postmark. Just a plain white six-by-nine envelope."

The same plain white envelope in which the printed photo had come to Grace, Rob realized. He withdrew his cell and pulled up the pic he'd taken. He showed it to Pierce. "An envelope like this one?"

Pierce nodded. "Exactly like that."

Rob showed the pic to Gibbons. "Whoever this guy's source is, he was already here."

There was always the possibility that more than one person was involved with Locke and his murder. That person or persons could also know Grace's identity because of their connection to Locke. The real question was how Locke had known. Grace had gone to great lengths to disappear and start a new life.

"Mr. Pierce," Gibbons said, "would you be willing to submit your fingerprints for the purpose of being ruled out of this investigation? I'm sure you're aware that the timing of your arrival and the information you have just provided makes you a person of interest."

Pierce looked from Gibbons to Rob and back. "I'll

make the two of you a deal. You allow me the exclusive on this story—however it plays out—and I'll give you my fingerprints, DNA, whatever you need."

"You have a deal, Mr. Pierce," Rob said before Gibbons could. "I'll call my CSI guy right now."

Gibbons nodded. "Works for me."

"Just one other question," Rob countered. "Have you reached any conclusions as to why your source sent you to this inn? There's lots of other lodging options in Chattanooga."

"You're here," he pointed out. "I'm guessing it has something to do with the owner. The timing of her purchase is within the past three years. She has a child the right age. It's an easy leap to the conclusion that she's the victim's former wife."

That he knew so much made Rob sick. He stood. "Excuse me, gentlemen. I'll make that call and get right back with you."

He needed to talk to Grace.

"I'm right, aren't I?" Pierce demanded.

Rob didn't bother with an answer. That was one for Grace and Grace alone.

In the kitchen, Liam was finishing his breakfast and watching cartoons on the small television that sat on the counter next to the refrigerator. Diane was busy cleaning up after her breakfast prep. Grace hovered near her son, looking as distraught as Rob imagined she felt.

Her gaze connected with his, and he didn't mince words. "Pierce is a freelance reporter from LA. I ran a background check on him last night."

Something like horror claimed her face. "How did he know to come?"

"He received a note in an envelope just like the one your photo arrived in. Delivered in a similar manner."

Her face paled. "So he *knows*."

Rob nodded. "He knows."

Chapter Nine

Grace's knees felt weak, and yet somehow, she managed to remain vertical.

If the man was a reporter and he knew her former identity—she refused to consider the past her true identity—then it was only a matter of time before the whole world would know.

"I—I can't..." Her gaze settled on her precious son. "I have to get him someplace safe until this is..."

Rob held up his hands to slow her down. "He's made a deal that we give him the exclusive and he cooperates. For now, this is under control."

Diane moved next to Grace. "How can you be sure?"

Grace was thankful someone had the presence of mind to ask the question.

"He's here for a story. An exclusive. This is important to him," Rob said. "We can control the narrative because we have the story."

Made sense, she supposed. "What about Mr. Brower?"

"He's here with a company planning an expansion into the Chattanooga area. He wants no part of this business."

Grace nodded. "My God, the man must be mortified at the idea of what's happening here."

"I think he's okay." Rob took a step closer. "Right now, my primary concern is for you and Liam."

"We appreciate that." Grace worked up a grateful smile.

"Deputy Reynolds is coming over for a couple of hours while I go home for clothes. Sergeant Snelling will be coming to take Mr. Pierce's prints. Gibbons wants to rule him out as a suspect in Locke's murder."

"If he's ruled out," Grace said, "which I suspect he will be, that means we're still looking for..."

Rob nodded. There was no need for her to go on with Liam in the room.

She felt an overwhelming urge to tell him and Diane about the keys in the refrigerator and the rolling pin in the oven. She'd already asked Diane about the pizza and she hadn't ordered it. The events were not unlike the breakdown Grace suffered after her father's death. But she couldn't bring it up...especially not now. Not with that reporter on the premises.

Diane patted her on the arm. "I'm canceling my yoga class today." She walked over to Liam. "Come on, buddy. You and I are having a party at your place."

"Yay! Can we play in the snow?"

"Maybe later, but not this morning," Grace answered for Diane.

"But we can build a Lego castle to the sky!" Diane teased as she grabbed him and headed for the door.

Grace had no idea how she would ever thank Diane enough. Or Rob. Her gaze shifted to him. "You don't know how much I appreciate all you're doing."

He held up his hands again. "No thanks necessary." He dropped his arms to his sides. "I have a couple of calls to make. Then I should confirm Gibbons and I are on the same page. You okay for a few minutes?"

"I am." She nodded. Forced a smile. "Thanks."

When he'd disappeared through that swinging door, Grace hugged herself. How would she ever feel comfortable in this life she'd carved out once everyone knew the truth? It wasn't that she felt she wouldn't be safe once Adam's killer was found. It was more about how this would affect Liam in the future. She hadn't wanted him to know this horrible truth. How could she protect him if everyone around them knew?

She drew in a big breath and gathered her resolve around her. For the moment, her choices were limited. Their immediate safety was paramount.

A knock at the back door made her jump. Her gaze landed on a face in the door's window, and Grace breathed a sigh of relief. Cara. Forcing a steadiness she did not feel, she walked to the door, unlocked and opened it.

"Sorry," Cara said. "I forgot my key."

"It's okay. I'm just a little jumpy this morning."

Cara hung her coat on one of the remaining hooks in the corner drop zone. Then she grabbed Grace in a hug. "Of course you are. I am so sorry all this is happening to you." She drew back. "Any news this morning?"

Where did Grace begin? "You mean besides the fact that Mr. Pierce is a reporter from LA who received a note telling him to come here?" Grace shivered, hugged her arms around herself again. "A note in an envelope exactly like the one that photo was in—the one someone had tucked into the mailbox."

"Oh my word, have they arrested him?" Cara hung her purse on the hook with her coat. "He could be the killer."

Grace shook her head. "At this point they think he was lured here by the killer." She drew in a big breath. "Or maybe Adam lured him here and then something went wrong."

Cara grabbed a mug and went to the coffeepot. "That's what I'm saying. Reporters can be pretty ruthless. Who knows why he came or what he's done since he got here."

"I'll ask Rob what he thinks when he gets back."

"Where's Liam?" Cara sipped her coffee.

"Diane took him to our space to play. It was getting a little tense in here." Grace frowned. "Did you order pizza for us last night?"

Cara made a face. "Pizza?"

Grace explained the delivery, and, like Diane, Cara had no idea who could have placed the order.

Another load of dread sagged Grace's shoulders. How could she order a pizza delivery and not remember? Her cell vibrated in her hip pocket, drawing her from the worry. She checked the screen. Paula. "Good morning, Paula. Is everything okay?"

Paula and Karl were usually here by now. Grace had been so caught up in the news about Pierce she hadn't noticed their absence.

"I'm headed to the urgent care with Karl. He woke up with a fever and a horrible headache this morning. I'm worried it's the flu."

"Oh, no. Please keep us posted and take care of yourselves. We'll be fine here."

The call ended, and Grace considered all that she would need to do with Paula not coming in. Maybe for a few days if they actually had the flu.

"Everything okay?"

Grace blinked. She really had to get her head on straight. She'd forgotten Cara was in the room. "Karl is sick. Paula thinks it may be the flu."

"All right, then." Cara finished off her coffee and put her cup in the sink. "That means I'm Paula today. You just let me know if you need anything."

Grace shook her head. "I can do Paula's work if you want to man the desk."

"No way," Cara said as she backed toward the door. "I'm the assistant. You're the boss."

Rather than argue, Grace finished the cleanup in the kitchen and then did the same in the dining room. She tidied the buffet, leaving the muffins and cookies. She loved the array of glass domes the former owners had collected. All shapes and sizes, making for the best displays.

She ran the sweeper over the dining room carpet before moving on to the registration desk. She wasn't expecting any new arrivals today, but there was always some sort of paperwork to be done. Or bills to pay.

On her way to the desk, she checked in on Liam. As promised, the Legos were climbing ever higher. She caught Diane up on the Wilborns and how Cara had volunteered to pick up the slack.

"I'll be at the desk whenever you're ready to send Liam my way."

Later, as she worked on some bills, Mr. Brower waved goodbye and hurried through the lobby, heading out for today's conference session. Grace was grateful to see he wasn't carrying his luggage. After the events of the past twenty-four hours, frankly, she was surprised he wasn't abandoning ship.

"Have a nice day," Grace called after him.

The temperature was higher today, which meant the snow would likely all melt away. It was too warm at this point for any ice on the roads. Good news on both counts, as far as Grace was concerned. She loved snow around Christmas, but she was over it well before February rolled around.

The bell over the front door rang, drawing her attention there. Deputy Reynolds walked in, looking far more chipper than a man who'd had surveillance duty until 2:00 a.m. should.

"Good morning," Grace said. "Thank you so much for your late stay last night."

"No problem." He glanced around the lobby. "I just wanted you to know that I'm here. Deputy Vaughn had to run home for a bit, but I'll be here until he re-turns."

"I appreciate that. There are fresh-baked muffins and cookies as well as coffee in the dining room."

Reynolds grinned. "You talked me into it."

The muffins had turned out especially well this morning. At least something had gone right.

The bell tinkled again. Grace propped a smile in place, expecting it to be Sergeant Snelling. Rob had said he would be stopping by.

Not Snelling.

The man in the jeans and puffer jacket strolled up to the desk. "Good morning. I'm Russell Ames. I have a reservation."

Grace tapped back her surprise. She hadn't taken any reservations for today. "One moment, Mr. Ames." She clicked the keys on her keyboard and scrolled the registry.

"Are you Ms. Myers?"

She looked up. "Yes. Grace Myers. Please call me Grace."

"Well, you were right, Grace. This mountain of yours is beautiful. The views from the inn are mag-nificent."

Grace bit back the words that rushed to the tip of her tongue. She had not spoken to this man. Had not taken his reservation. Her gaze slid back down to the screen and there it was—the reservation. Her initials were there as well.

No. This couldn't be right.

"Is everything okay?" Mr. Ames asked.

She nodded quickly. "Yes."

Struggling to keep her hands from shaking, she completed the check-in. "Almost all done. I'll just need your credit card."

When he provided the card, she tucked it into the machine and waited for it to process. With that out of the way, she assigned him a room and handed him the key.

"You may park anywhere you like," she said, barely keeping a smile pinned in place. "Breakfast and dinner are provided with your stay. Lunch is optional. Your key fits your room as well as the front door. We do lock up by midnight."

"Great." He hitched a thumb toward the door. "I'll grab my suitcase."

She watched him go, thankful he wasn't from California too.

How could she have made a reservation, chatted with the man, and not remember it? Did she have to ask? She vividly recalled those moments the last time when she slowly began to realize something was very wrong. The worst moment had been when she'd started into town and realized the baby wasn't with her. She'd left him at home, sleeping.

What kind of mother left her baby at home alone in his crib while she drove away?

A mother who had gone over the edge from all the stress.

Was she hovering on that ledge again?

She finished up with the paperwork and decided she needed to check on Liam. When she walked into the room, Diane was straightening the mess Liam had created with his big build.

"He passed out." Diane cocked her head toward the sofa.

Liam was asleep there. He rarely took morning naps anymore. He must have tuckered himself out playing, and besides, he had gotten to bed late last night.

"Thank you," she said to her friend. "I really appreciate everything."

"Not a problem at all. In fact," she said as she stood, "I think if you're good here, I'll run to the market and pick up those pork chops I ordered. Remember they were out when I went the other day?"

"Are we having pork chops tonight?" Grace felt a new twinge of worry that she didn't remember Diane mentioning the market being out.

"We are," she said. "I have a new recipe I think will be the best ever."

"Your recipes are all the best ever," Grace assured her.

"See you in half an hour or so."

She was off. Grace draped a thin blanket over her boy and walked back to the desk, leaving the door open and turning on the app on her phone.

The front entrance warned of a new arrival as she entered the lobby. This time it was Sergeant Snelling.

"Morning, Grace," he said.

Snelling was a tall, broad-shouldered man who stood at least six-three or -four. A little gray peppered his dark hair. His smile was as wide as his shoulders, and he was very kind. She'd only met him once at a big community picnic for July Fourth. Rob had made sure she was introduced around that day. Like everyone else Grace had met since moving here, Snelling was a very nice man.

"Good morning. Deputy Reynolds is here grabbing a coffee and fresh-baked muffin. Would you like to join him in the dining room?"

"I surely would."

Grace led him to the dining room and gave the two the cabin number for Mr. Pierce. They would be seeing him after their coffee and muffins.

A chill had penetrated the lobby, she noted as she returned to the desk. Though it was supposed to be warmer today, it was still plenty cool enough to keep a fire going. This was something she generally started as soon as she got up each morning. Likewise, she made sure it was out for the night when she went to bed.

She added a few logs, stirred the embers to get the flames going. This was a part of the job she would never dread. Her father had kept a fire going all winter when she was growing up. Maybe it was the scent of wood burning or the warmth or maybe just the ambience. But it reminded her of her father and her childhood. She wanted Liam to have those kinds of memories. The hard part appeared to be keeping all the ugliness at bay. Making that happen was getting harder every minute.

She thought of the reporter and what he would no

doubt write about her and her son. Whatever it was, it was not going to bode well for their future.

Unable to help herself, she checked in once more to see that Liam was still sleeping.

The blanket lay on the floor and the spot where he'd been lying was empty.

Grace's heart rushed into her throat. "Liam?"

She hurried into her bedroom. No Liam. Then she ran to his room and to the bathroom. No Liam. She called his name over and over. Checked under and behind every single thing.

Where was he?

Something in the yard beyond the window caught her attention.

Her breath caught. There he was...playing in the last of the melting snow.

"Liam!"

She rushed to the kitchen and out the back door. "Liam!"

Her beautiful little boy looked up at her. He wore his boots and his jacket but not his gloves or his hat.

"What're you doing out here?"

She reached for him, drew him into her arms. He was cold. His hands and boots were muddy from the melting snow.

"You told me I play in the snow."

"No, Liam," she said, heading back toward the door. "I did not tell you it was okay to come outside alone and play in the snow."

He nodded firmly, tears welling in his eyes. "Did too."

Her own tears burning her eyes, she opted not to argue with him. All that mattered was that he was okay.

"Come on. We'll get some fresh clothes and warm up."

She carried him close to her chest and didn't put him down until they were in his room. She fished out clean sweatpants with a dinosaur sweatshirt, and fresh socks. As he shed his boots and wet clothes, she barely suppressed the need to scream in frustration.

He had to have misunderstood when he'd asked her earlier, in the kitchen, about playing in the snow.

"Liam, remember when you were watching television and you asked me about playing in the snow and I said maybe later but not this morning?"

"Yep. Yep."

"When I said *maybe later*, it didn't mean *yes*."

He peered up at her, his eyes big. "You waked me up on the couch and said go outside play."

Disbelief slammed into her chest. "What?"

"You said go outside, Liam. Play in snow!"

Okay. It was possible he'd dreamed this. "How about next time you wait for Mommy to go with you? Is that a good idea?"

"Yep." He nodded enthusiastically.

When he was dressed and his soiled clothes were in the hamper, Grace selected a new sweater for herself. Though her jeans had survived without getting muddy or wet, her sweater hadn't. She brushed her hair, decided she was too tired to do her usual braid. Over the past two years it had become her trademark style. Not fancy or even trendy, but it worked. Just like her normal jeans and a sweater during the cool months and a simple blouse in the warm ones.

Grace would never be accused of being stylish, and that was okay with her.

The sound of someone coming through the main entrance had her heading in that direction. Liam had resumed his Lego creation, so she left the door open and confirmed the app was still on. She really should have heard him leave the room before. And she surely would have heard someone speaking to him, because it certainly wasn't her. Why hadn't she?

But could she be certain? The dread tightened her throat.

The idea occurred to her that the back door should have been locked in any event. Had Diane forgotten to lock it when she left?

In the lobby, Rob waited for her.

His hair was still a little damp from his shower, his jaw shaved clean, his uniform fresh. "Snelling is here already?"

"He and Reynolds went to cabin 10 to see Mr. Pierce. Maybe fifteen minutes ago."

She hesitated, wondered if she should tell him the things she appeared to be forgetting. Probably she should tell him everything about her breakdown and how she was feeling a little—maybe a lot—like that again.

The French doors that led onto the back of the property and the guest cabins suddenly burst open. Reynolds rushed in, nearly running in his hurry.

"Pierce is gone."

Rob frowned. "But there are two rentals in the lot. I saw them when I came in."

"We have a new guest," Grace said. "He's driving a rental."

"Well, damn." To Reynolds, Rob said, "Get the license plate from Grace and put out an APB. Where's Snelling?"

"Still at Pierce's cabin." Reynolds looked from Rob to Grace and back. "The door was standing open."

Grace wanted to yell or kick something. What the hell? Adam was dead. And now the Los Angeles reporter who had also received an anonymous message was missing.

What was next?

Or better yet, *who* was next?

"I have to check on Liam." She ran back to her room. Found her son right where she'd left him.

Grace collapsed on the sofa, the tears spilling past her lashes however hard she tried to hold them back.

It felt like she was back there, two years and eight months ago. Falling apart and wholly dependent on the one and only person left to take care of her and her child.

"Grace."

She turned to the door where Deputy Reynolds lingered. Oh, God, she'd forgotten he needed the license plate number.

"I'm sorry." She stood, swiped at the damned tears. "Can you stay here with Liam while I get that for you?"

"Course I can." Reynolds walked over to where Liam worked and crouched down. "Wow, that's the most amazing Lego tower I've ever seen."

Grace went to the desk, opened the registration software and pulled up the information on Pierce. But his rental car information was missing.

"Wait." She closed the software and reopened it. There was no way she would have failed to enter the information. A license plate was required to register.

Still, the space was filled with zeros. Empty boxes would not have allowed the program to save and close, but the zeros did the trick.

Shaking her head, she closed it out and stormed back to her parlor, where Reynolds waited. "The information is missing."

He pushed to his feet. "Missing?"

She explained what she meant. "It had to have been deleted."

At hearing the shift in his mother's tone, Liam looked up, worry shadowing his sweet face.

Grace drew in a deep breath and reached for calm. "Could you let Deputy Vaughn know I need to speak with him?"

Reynolds nodded. "Sure thing. I'll go tell him now."

She had made a promise to herself that she would never tell anyone about those horrible, horrible weeks that had turned into months after her father's death... after the police had harassed her relentlessly. She had fallen completely apart. If not for the help of Val, she would surely have lost her son and maybe her life.

The media had already printed accusations that any woman who lived with a murderer and claimed not to recognize what he was wasn't operating on all cylinders, or maybe she was just as evil as he was.

But she hadn't been crazy or evil. She had been naive. She had believed the man she loved.

She had made a mistake. And that mistake had cost her everything she cared about, except her son.

She could not lose her son.

Chapter Ten

Joe Pierce had split or he'd been abducted. Either option was bad.

Fury cut through Rob, and he wanted to punch something.

What the hell was the guy up to? He'd admitted he received a note that told him to come here, had agreed to be fingerprinted, and now he'd just disappeared?

It didn't look good for Pierce.

"No sign of foul play other than the door being open," Gibbons said, surveying the room. "His bags are still here." He nodded to the suitcase and carry-on bag on the bench at the foot of the bed.

"We've put out a BOLO." Since Grace hadn't been able to pull up the info on his rental car, they hadn't been able to provide a description of the vehicle just yet. "I'm hoping we'll get a quick response from anyone who's seen him."

"I say," Gibbons suggested, "we lift some prints from this room to compare with any you've collected at the Cashion scene."

"Already in the works," Rob assured him. "Sergeant Snelling called in another of his investigators."

Maybe Gibbons thought a small town wouldn't be able to keep up with his big-city way of doing things, but he would be wrong.

"We're in your jurisdiction," Gibbons said. "You could call in the FBI if you felt you needed the assist."

"You didn't call them in when you were working on the Locke case the first time," Rob countered.

"I did call them. But the support I got was minimal. The only things we knew back then," Gibbons said, "was that three women had gone missing in the span of two years, and all three ended up dead with a heart-shaped locket on a chain wrapped around their left hands. Same manner of death—tortured, stabbed in the heart, and then over and over for whatever reason. We found no matching cases in the databases we checked. The Bureau gave us a profile that turned out to be pretty accurate, but that was about the extent of what we got. We just didn't have enough to tie what we'd found to anyone or any trail left behind in any other case. It was a dead end."

"Until," Rob said, "Locke's wife found a woman in the basement of their home."

Rob had done his research. The details of the case had sickened him. All three victims, four including the one Grace had freed from the basement and who was later found murdered, fit a particular profile. Blond hair, pale eyes—either blue or gray—and petite. He hadn't realized until he'd done his research that Grace fit the profile as well. She obviously kept her hair dyed brown for that reason. He hadn't known it wasn't her natural color until he saw the images of her from the news during Locke's arrest nearly three years ago.

He couldn't even conceive how those memories haunted her. That part of her life had been a nightmare—the things horror flicks were made of.

Gibbons walked to the window. "At least he got what was coming to him in the end. I'm just sorry I wasn't here to witness it."

Rob's gaze narrowed. "This case is personal for you."

"He has that handful of followers—fans," Gibbons said, his attention fixed on the backyard. "They harassed my family for all those months as the case built toward trial. Killed our dog." He exhaled a big breath. "You have no idea how badly I wish I could have caught the son of a bitch who did that. And then, just as we're finally going to trial, Locke gets to walk. Like nothing happened."

Rob felt for the guy. "Like you said, he got his. It's the follower or followers we have to worry about now. Do you think Pierce is one of his followers? He wasn't on your radar during the initial arrest or more recently as the trial was about to start?"

Gibbons turned to face him. "I've never seen him before. Never heard of him. Doesn't mean he isn't one of them."

"Locke had that many followers?" Rob would never understand how people could become obsessed with killers, but it happened. More often than not.

A shrug lifted the older detective's shoulders. "Not so many, really. Maybe a half dozen who showed up in person to protest outside the courthouse when he was arraigned. But there was someone who was involved with him or worked closely with him. All the indicators were there, but we were never able to pinpoint anyone."

Rob got it now. "You thought it was Grace."

"His wife, yes. She was with him all that time. They were expecting a child together. I assumed she was protecting her family in a twisted sort of way."

No way would Grace ever do anything like that. "But you were wrong."

Gibbons hesitated, then nodded slowly. "I suppose I was."

It annoyed Rob immensely that the man didn't sound entirely convinced.

"In the end, what really killed the case was my mistake," Gibbons admitted. "I wanted solid evidence—the foolproof kind. I knew the only way to ensure we got it was to go into that house before Locke or whoever was helping him could get back in there and maybe destroy evidence. Bella Watts, another woman who fit the Locke profile, had gone missing just days before, so I used the possibility that she could be in that house for exigent circumstances. When Watts was found, a couple weeks after Locke's arrest, I knew that damned search would come back to haunt us. Nothing I could do about it then."

"So Watts wasn't one of his victims?" Rob had

been curious about how a seasoned detective could make such a mistake regarding the search.

Gibbons considered the question for a moment. "I'll always believe she was—she fit his MO perfectly. But her throat was slit, her body dumped unceremoniously in an alley."

"Damn." Rob could understand the man's pain.

Reynolds appeared at the door. "Ms. Myers needs to see you," he said to Rob.

"We have someone from Snelling's team headed this way," Rob said, before exiting. "Make sure he understands we need a comparison with the prints taken from the Cashion place ASAP."

"You got it," Reynolds assured him.

Rob was grateful for an excuse to get back to Grace. He really tried to see Gibbons's side of things, but considering most of his conclusions put Grace on the wrong side of the issues, Rob was having trouble with the idea.

Grace was staring out a window in the lobby—the same one where Liam had seen the man looking in at him. The laughter coming from down the hall told him Cara was with the boy. A clatter of pans from farther down the hall suggested Diane was in the kitchen, maybe prepping for dinner or just putting together lunch. No sign of the newest guest to arrive.

Rob joined Grace at the window.

"Did you find Pierce?" she asked.

"He's not in his cabin, but his bags are still there. All we know for the moment is that he's MIA."

She shook her head. "I don't want my son touched by all this, and I have no idea how to stop it."

He reached for her hand, gave it a squeeze before letting go. She stared up at him, her eyes full of worry. "I'm sorry this has come here—to this community. I really thought I'd outrun my past."

"Locke's gone," Rob reminded her. "He will never bother you again. Once we pinpoint whoever was helping him or following him, it'll be over."

"I need to tell you what happened to me after he was arrested. After I'd made my statement and gone home to settle my father's affairs."

Rob glanced around. "Why don't we go into your office."

She looked confused, then nodded as if she'd realized what he meant. She was badly shaken, no question about that.

She led the way to the small office behind the registration desk. The room had originally been a coat closet since at one time the inn had hosted enormous dinners. He leaned against the doorframe so he could see any comings and goings in the lobby.

Grace stood in the center of the small room as if she couldn't decide whether to sit or to pace.

Finally, she said, "I had a breakdown. Liam was only three months old and I fell apart. My father's longtime house manager, a member of the family, really—Valentina Hicks—was like my surrogate mother after my mom died. She took care of everything, including me, all my life, while my father was at work and then later, when I fell apart. She took me to her home near Truckee. She cared for me until I was well enough to get away and start over."

The story gripped his chest like a vise. "If anyone ever had a reason to fall apart," he offered, "you certainly did."

She folded her arms over her chest. "You don't understand. I mean I fell apart completely. I couldn't remember anything. I kept misplacing things—even my baby. I stopped eating. Taking care of myself. I was a mess."

"I get it. It was bad. I still say you had every right."

"I suppose so." She looked away. "But I think it's happening again now."

He considered the ramifications of her admission for a moment. "How so?"

"I had no idea I'd made a reservation for Mr. Ames. I've put my keys in the refrigerator—my rolling pin in the oven. Pizza was ordered using my cell phone. Mr. Pierce's license plate number was left off his reservation or removed later. And the real heart-stopper—I woke Liam up from a nap this morning and told him he could go outside and play."

Worry twisted his gut. "You found him outside playing?"

She nodded. "I asked why he went outside, and he said I woke him up and told him he could."

"Maybe he dreamed it." Damn. No wonder she was upset.

"I thought the same thing, but when you consider all the other little things, I'm…" She drew in a breath. "I'm terrified. I need to know that my son is safe, and now I'm worried I can't trust myself to make that happen."

"I'll be here," he promised.

"You were here today," she argued.

"But I didn't know you needed me in that way. I do now."

"No matter what else happens," she urged, "I need to know Liam is safe."

"You have my word, Grace."

"Thank you." She crossed the narrow space that stood between them and hugged him. "You have no idea how much that means to me."

The warmth her touch sent coursing through him had him wanting to do more than comfort her. But he resisted. Instead, he put his arms around her and hugged her back. "We've got this."

She drew back and smiled, though it was impossible to miss the emotion shining in her eyes. "Liam and I have felt at home here, and I don't want to lose that."

"There's something you should know, Grace."

Her smile faded and the worry that filled her eyes told him she expected the worst.

"It's not about all this," he assured her. "It's about me."

Her expression shifted to an expectant one. "Is something going on I should know about?"

"I've been meaning to ask you out to dinner or a movie again—" he shrugged "—something simple, for weeks now, but I kept putting it off. You didn't seem interested."

She grinned. "Well, you're wrong, Deputy Vaughn.

I'm very interested, and if the idea still holds appeal for you, let's revisit the possibility as soon as all this is over."

"Deal." He leaned down and brushed his lips across hers in the briefest of kisses before drawing away.

She pressed her forehead to his chin. "That was very nice."

He resisted the urge to do it again. "I should get back to work."

She stepped back. "Me too."

When they exited the office, Gibbons was coming from the kitchen, his expression grim.

"We need to talk," Gibbons said.

GRACE'S HEART SANK. The warmth generated by Rob's words and that quick kiss vanished. She was afraid to ask what had happened now. "I should check on Liam."

"You'll need to join us once you're done," Gibbons said to her.

Grace nodded and went on her way. In the parlor, Cara and Liam were watching a movie. Cara glanced up and smiled. "Everything okay?"

Grace wasn't sure everything would ever be okay again. Rather than say as much, she plastered on a smile and gave a nod. "You two having fun?"

"Shh," Liam whispered. "We missing best part."

Grace smiled and motioned to her lips as if she were zipping them. From there she went to the kitchen.

Diane held out a tray with sandwiches and veggie chips. "I thought everyone could use some food."

"I can take it to the dining room. Deputy Vaughn and Detective Gibbons are meeting there. I've been asked to join them."

"Did they find him—that Pierce guy?"

"He's not in his cabin and his car is gone. But his luggage is still here. He just disappeared despite knowing that he was supposed to meet with Rob this morning for fingerprints. Add to that the fact that his door was standing open, and it doesn't look good."

"Maybe he left the door open to make it look like foul play when really he had something to hide and didn't want to be fingerprinted." Diane shook her head, gave a shrug. "This just keeps getting better."

"For sure," Grace agreed.

Diane reached out and gave Grace's arm a squeeze. "We'll get through this."

Grace managed a smile. "Hope so."

Diane turned back to the recipe book she held.

"Did you find everything you needed at the market?"

"I did." She tapped the page she'd opened the book to. "We'll see how it turns out. This is a new entrée for me."

"I'm sure it will be amazing." She hitched her thumb toward the door. "I should get in there."

Dread making each step a burden, Grace carried the laden tray to the dining room. Rob immediately rushed over to take it from her.

"Diane made lunch," she announced.

After Grace offered drinks, she joined the two lawmen, choosing the chair closest to Rob.

"I made a few calls about this Joe Pierce," Gibbons said. "Turns out he got himself into some trouble about ten years ago. He was an *LA Times* reporter back then. He was working on a story—the Hollywood Hills Hunter."

Grace remembered that one. A serial killer had been stalking young women during early-morning runs. He'd killed four before he was caught. "I was a senior at UCLA then."

Gibbons nodded as if he'd already known exactly where she was at the time. He probably did. He'd investigated every part of her life when Adam was arrested. It was as if she had been the criminal.

"There was a young woman, also a senior at a local university," Gibbons went on. "Pierce hired her to run a particular route every morning in hopes of luring this killer. She wound up almost getting killed and Pierce was fired from the *Times*. He wasn't heard from for quite a while, which I suppose is why he started the freelance gig. No reputable paper was going to hire him after pulling a stunt like that."

Grace didn't recall any of those details. She must have been too caught up in exams. "Does this have something to do with the Locke case?"

"I hoped you could answer that for me."

Grace looked from Gibbons to Rob and back. "I don't know what you mean."

"Did you know Pierce back then? The LA detective I spoke with says there was another woman working with Pierce to lure the Hollywood Hills Hunter."

"No." Grace drew back as if he'd thrown something at her. "I've never met the man before. Never even heard of him."

"What exactly are you accusing Grace of?" Rob demanded, his tone just shy of heated.

"I'm not accusing her of anything," Gibbons argued. "I'm only trying to establish a connection. Pierce shows up here—apparently invited by the same person who left a note for you. It feels like there should have been a connection to you."

"Well, you're wrong," Grace said flatly. "I've never met him."

Reynolds appeared at the door. "Vaughn, can I speak with you a moment?"

"Give me a minute." Rob stood and glanced at Grace. "Don't answer any other questions until I'm back."

She nodded her understanding. Clearly Gibbons was determined to connect all of this to her one way or another.

Gibbons waited until Rob and Deputy Reynolds were out of earshot. "I'm not trying to accuse you of anything, Gia."

"Grace," she reminded him. "And it sounds as if that's exactly what you're doing."

"No," he argued. "I only want to get to the truth. Locke is dead, and I, for one, am glad. But whoever came here with him—whoever killed him—I want that person too. As I'm sure you do as well. You must know you're not safe as long as his killer is out there doing God knows what."

There was nothing to say. Unquestionably she understood the situation. The fact that he insisted he felt the same way she did didn't make her trust him.

Rob came back into the dining room. Right behind him was Deputy Reynolds and Diane.

Grace sat up straighter. Why had Diane been drawn into this uncomfortable situation? That she wouldn't look at Grace had a cold knot forming in her belly.

Rob looked to Grace. "There's been a development, but Diane has asked to tell you about it herself."

Grace clutched her hands together, hoped this wasn't going to be even worse news. "Diane, are you all right?"

Diane nodded. "Before I lived in New York," she began, "I lived in Los Angeles. I was a copy editor for the *LA Times*."

Grace tensed. The idea of where this was going made her want to run from the room before Diane could say another word.

"My boyfriend was an up-and-coming reporter hell-bent on making a name for himself." She closed her eyes a moment. "Joe Pierce."

Grace's hand went to her mouth. *No.*

"He was a jerk." She shrugged, still not looking at Grace. "And when I found out he'd hired this college kid to help him try to lure a killer, I was furious. I dumped him. But the worst part is, the girl was someone I'd introduced him to. She'd spent a few weeks interning with me. Anyway, I left and never looked back. And I never heard from him again. Apparently, he'd been following my blog the past few years and realized I was in this area. When he received that anonymous note, he thought I'd sent it to him. He caught me at the market this morning, and we had a terrible argument in the parking lot. I accused him of trying to use me again to get to a story. But he swears he only came because of the note and because he thought I was the one who sent it."

Maybe Grace was a fool twice over, but she believed Diane. "Thank you for telling me. I know you would never do anything to hurt Liam or me. I'm certain this is just as you said."

"Diane," Rob said, his attention focused on Gibbons, "has been living in the area for a year now. There have been zero complaints about her."

"I was already living in New York when the Locke case happened," she hastened to add. She turned to Grace then. "And you're right. I would never do anything to harm you or Liam. That's why Pierce and I argued at the market. I wanted to know what the hell he was doing here and what his intentions were. He only said he'd been invited."

Grace suppressed a shudder and somehow managed to work up a smile for her friend. "Thank you for trying to protect us."

"I believe," Gibbons said then, "that it would be best if you, Diane, and the other employees of the inn remained here until this situation is straightened out. At this point we don't know who or what we're dealing with. It will be easier to see that everyone is protected if we're all here together."

"I agree," Grace said. "If that's all right with you," she added, looking to Diane.

Diane nodded. "Whatever I need to do."

Grace made a face. "Wait. That may be a problem for Cara. She sees after her elderly grandmother." Grace remembered the call from Paula. "And the Wilborns are home with the flu, so they'll need to stay put."

"Very well." Gibbons stood. "We'll talk again when we have more information."

"We're awaiting fingerprint analysis from the crime scene where Locke's body was found," Rob explained.

Gibbons looked from Grace to Diane and then to Rob. "I'm sure you will all be happy to provide your prints for comparison."

The silence in the room was deafening.

Chapter Eleven

The guests—except for Pierce—had wandered into the dining room. Grace had insisted that Rob tell his deputies to stop by as they were able and have dinner. They were all working overtime because of her. It was the least she could do.

Gibbons had left after Sergeant Snelling collected Grace's, Cara's and Diane's prints. Rob had told him not to bother the Wilborns under the circumstances. The couple had lived in the area for decades. To ask for their prints in this situation was ludicrous.

Grace watched Liam ride the tricycle he'd only just learned to pedal around the lobby. He'd gotten very good at avoiding the furniture. Her heart lifted watching him play as if the world weren't crumbling around them. She was so thankful for his innocent bliss.

The blaze of the fire on the far side of the room somehow gave her comfort. She remembered seeing that massive stone fireplace for the first time and how it had reminded her so much of the one at her father's home in Lake Tahoe. She had known then that this was the place she and Liam would call home.

How had everything fallen apart so fast?

Because of Adam. Anger, hatred and frustration roared inside her. Even in death he tormented her.

She pushed the thought away and focused on the upcoming weekend's calendar. Two more guests were arriving on Friday. She sure hoped this was over by then, but she had a terrible feeling it wouldn't be.

The phone rang and she answered with the usual greeting. "The Lookout Inn."

"Hello. Grace Myers, please," the male voice said.

Grace braced for trouble, no matter that she received calls like this all the time. "This is she."

"Hello, this is Allen Warren of Warren Hardscapes. I'm calling to confirm our start date of Monday, the twenty-sixth, for your project. I'll need to stop by tomorrow and pick up your deposit."

Grace went stone still. "I'm sorry—who is this again?"

"Allen Warren," he repeated. "I did an estimate a few weeks ago for a backyard redo at your inn. You agreed to the estimate and we scheduled the start date—the twenty-sixth."

"I—I'm sorry. I have no idea about this. Are you sure it was me you spoke with?"

"Ms. Myers," he said, his tone going firm, "I don't know what's going on, but I've scheduled my entire team on your job for five days. I have other customers who are waiting."

"I'm really sorry, Mr. Warren." Her heart was pounding now. "If you can just give me some time to sort this out… Perhaps you can move one of your other customers up and then we can discuss this further. Right now, there's an official police investigation at the inn."

She hated, hated, to resort to using a murder investigation as an excuse, but she didn't know what else to do.

The dead air on the other end had her tension escalating.

"All right. I'll contact you next week to reschedule. Meanwhile, I suggest you review your contract. Good evening, Ms. Myers."

The call ended.

Grace placed the handset back in its cradle and quickly searched her computer for anything related to Warren Hardscapes. Her heart dropped when she discovered a string of emails, including a digitally signed contract for more than twenty thousand dollars in exterior work.

Her fingers numb, she closed out of the emails and shut off the computer. It would be nice to update the rear patio areas, that was true, but she hadn't anticipated doing it this year. She could scratch up the necessary payment. It would drain her working capital, but there was a contract. She had little choice. Unless she could prove there had been a mistake. Moving on autopilot, she stepped from behind the desk and walked over to where Liam had stopped riding and was pretending to work on his tricycle.

The little plastic tools he kept in the basket made her smile. He so loved watching Karl Wilborn work on the lawn mower. For two years now, Grace had felt comfortable and safe here. She'd thought nothing of allowing anyone on her staff to see after Liam. Now, suddenly everyone around her was a suspect. Not in her eyes—not really, she insisted—but in the eyes of the law.

Would this nightmare ever be over?

The bell tinkled, heralding an arrival. Grace turned to see who'd walked in. There were no new guests scheduled, as far as she recalled, which wasn't saying much.

Detective Gibbons.

He was back.

She'd expected he would return eventually, but a part of her had hoped never to see him again. Ha ha. Like that was going to happen anytime soon.

"We need a private meeting, *Ms. Myers*," he said without preamble, his expression more smug than usual. "Is Deputy Vaughn here?"

Grace swallowed at the lump that rose in her throat. She wanted to ask what now, but she wasn't sure she wanted to know. Whatever it was, it couldn't be good. Nothing associated with this man and her past was good.

"He's in the kitchen talking to his deputies." She reached for Liam. "Come along, sweetie. We need to find Miss Diane or Miss Cara."

Gibbons walked quickly toward the kitchen. Grace watched him go; her heart had already started to pound. The way he'd called her Ms. Myers and the knowing look on his face spelled trouble for her.

She and Liam found Diane in the reading parlor. She was putting books back on shelves and tidying magazines.

"Is it okay if Liam stays with you for a bit?" Grace felt terrible having to constantly put her son off on others, but she was reasonably certain that nothing Gibbons had to say would be good for Liam to hear.

"Of course." Diane held out her hand. "Come along, my little friend, and we'll find that book you love so much."

Liam's eyes lit up. "Berry tales!"

"That's right." Diane grinned. "Fairy tales."

Close enough, Grace thought. Her son was never at a loss for answers or words, even if he had to make them up.

Grace closed the double pocket doors as she exited the parlor. She hurried to the main hall and then to the kitchen. The deputies were all gone, except Rob and, of course, Gibbons. Cara was loading the dishwasher.

Grace was so thankful for these women. They were true friends.

Rob smiled and gave her a nod. To Gibbons he said, "Grace and I need a moment."

Gibbons waved his hand as if to approve the request.

Anger stirred inside her, pushing aside some of the other emotions tugging at her.

Rob touched her elbow, guiding her from the room. He didn't stop until they had reached her private quarters. Inside, door closed, she said, "I'm almost afraid to ask what's happened now."

"Let's sit down," Rob offered.

The fear was back with force. She shook her head. "Just tell me, Rob."

"The fingerprint comparisons came back with one match."

She held her breath. Prayed that the people she adored—the people she trusted—were not somehow caught up in the bastard's murder.

"You."

Grace blinked. "What?"

"Your prints were found at the Cashion crime scene."

No. "That's impossible. I don't even know where they live beyond what you told me. How could I have been there?" This was crazy!

"That's exactly what I said," Rob said. "There were only three prints belonging to you. I've asked Snelling to further analyze them to determine if they were forged."

This was too much. "What does that mean? Forged?"

"There are techniques a person can use to lift prints from a surface and then to transfer them to another. It's not that difficult. The difficulty lies in making them look authentic. Some people and some techniques are better than others. These, according to Gibbons, are very good."

Hope flared. "Then he knows my prints were, as you say, forged. I wasn't at the crime scene."

"He knows that's a possibility because I told him

your being there was impossible." He exhaled a breath, shook his head. "Until Snelling gets back to us with a call one way or the other, Gibbons can act on what he has. He's gone over my head and requested a search warrant for the inn and the grounds."

"Can he do that?"

Rob nodded slowly. "I spoke to the sheriff a few minutes ago. She called me right before Gibbons arrived to warn me about what was going down. I told him you would be more than happy to cooperate with a search."

"Of course." She shook her head. "It's the prints I can't get past. I was not there."

"I know you weren't. But the quickest way to defuse this is to cooperate. You have nothing to hide."

Grace felt suddenly sick. "Something else happened." God, she hated to tell him this. He believed in her. She wanted to believe in herself, but that confidence was slipping. Through the tightness in her throat, she told him about the call from Warren Hardscapes. "I found the contract in my email. It looks as if I made the deal and scheduled the work."

"Did you talk about possibly doing landscape work with anyone?"

"Sure." She shrugged. "I've talked all about the things around here I'd like to do to anyone who'd listen." Everything was crashing down around her. "I don't know what to think anymore." She fixed her gaze on his. "At what point do I admit that maybe I've already lost control and I'm having blackouts or something like that?" Her heart sank with the words.

His strong fingers closed gently around her arms. "We take this one step at a time, one issue at a time. Right now, the search and your prints are the most pressing ones. This other stuff will have to wait its turn. Like I told you, I'm here. I'm not going to let you down."

She wondered how long it would be before he understood what an error he had made trusting her.

She took a deep breath. "Okay. I've put Mr. Warren off for now."

"Good. Let's deal with Gibbons. He and two of my deputies will conduct the search, and then we'll see what happens next. Snelling will get back to me as soon as he's confirmed the prints were forged."

He stated it all so confidently.

Grace hoped he was right.

9:00 p.m.

ROB STATIONED REYNOLDS in the kitchen with Grace and Cara. Diane was with Liam watching television. Rob followed every step Gibbons made. He ensured every single thing touched was put back exactly as it had been found.

The only rooms or cabins off-limits were those currently occupied—except for Pierce's. He remained AWOL, so his room was fair game.

Thankfully, by the time they returned to the lobby to start the search of the common areas, the other two guests were either in their room for the night or out for the evening.

The lobby went relatively fast, as did the reading parlor and the office. Grace's quarters took some time. Liam and Diane had moved to the reading parlor to play hide-and-seek. It was past the kid's bedtime, but until they were finished with the private quarters, Diane would need to keep him occupied.

Rob had to grit his teeth when the search through Grace's closet and dresser drawers went down. He didn't like anyone—not even his deputies—touching her private things. He'd wanted to offer to search her quarters, but he'd known Gibbons would never let him. He had figured out Rob had a soft spot for Grace. What he had was a lot more than that, but it was none of the man's business.

A deep breath was impossible until they were out of Grace's bedroom. By the time they'd exited her private space, he was ready to go off on Gibbons. The man had to see that Grace was innocent. Why was he making this harder on her than necessary? He should be glad Locke was dead.

Except Rob knew what he was after. He was still stinging from the idea that someone had given Locke help before his arrest as well as after. He believed that someone was Grace, but there was no way that was true.

Rob trusted her. He believed in her. Whatever she had missed before Locke's arrest, she would not have helped him after. There was no way she'd put Liam's future at risk. No way.

They moved to the dining room and finally to the kitchen.

"I'd like the deputies to get started out back," Gibbons said. "I'll finish up in here."

Rob gave Reynolds and Carter a nod and the two headed out the back door. The outside space wouldn't take that long. There was an old shed but it wasn't that large. The rest was mostly open space with flower beds and seating areas, then the bluff that overlooked the valley below. An iron fence crossed the property at the bluff line.

It was well past dark, so seeing anything beyond that six-foot iron fence would be impossible.

Grace and Cara stood at the island, arms crossed over their chests, and watched as Gibbons checked each cupboard and drawer, the appliances…every damned thing.

When he'd stopped searching and stood surveying the room at large, Rob asked, "Seen enough?"

Gibbons made a face, then turned back to the sink. He crouched down and opened the doors beneath it. He'd already dug around under there once.

Cara shook her head. "This is ridiculous."

Grace looked horrified.

Rob wished he could save her from all this nonsense.

Gibbons stood, a box of cleaning pads in his gloved hand. He placed the box on the island and peered inside the open flaps. He looked up at Grace, something almost sinister in his expression.

Then he reached inside and pulled out a plastic bag.

The bag was dark… No… Rob's heart skipped a beat. It was rust colored.

Bloody.

Gibbons placed the bag on the counter. Rob moved closer. Inside the gallon-sized locking storage bag was a fixed blade knife.

With a bloodied handle and bloodied blade.

"What's this, Ms. Myers?" Gibbons asked, his narrowed gaze focused on his prey.

Rob felt sick. This was not good.

"I have no idea," Grace said, her head moving from side to side.

The back door burst open and Reynolds stood in the doorway. "Rob, you need to come outside."

The look of dread on his deputy's face, combined with the fact that he'd called him Rob, warned that there was something really bad outside as well.

Gibbons whirled on Reynolds. "What did you find?"

Reynolds glanced at Grace and Cara. "It's the missing guy. Pierce. He's in the shed. He's been stabbed multiple times." He glanced at Grace again before lighting his gaze on Rob once more. "Like the other victim."

"Call Snelling," Rob said, his voice far steadier than he'd expected. "And the ME. I'll be right there."

Reynolds gave a nod and went back outside, closing the door behind him.

"Well, Deputy Vaughn," Gibbons said, "I think we have ourselves a dilemma here." He set his attention on Grace. "Are we going to find your prints on this knife and with this dead man?"

"The shed is on her property," Rob said, his fury building once more. "Of course her prints—real ones—will likely be there."

Gibbons shook his head. "I know you don't want to see this, but how do you explain what I suspect is the murder weapon being under the sink?"

"I have no idea how it got there," Grace fairly shouted at the man. "I've never seen that knife before."

"Even though you apparently used it on your ex-husband?" Gibbons demanded.

"No!" Grace fell back a step as if his words had pushed her.

"Grace," Rob warned. "Don't say anything else." She stared at him as if he'd landed a blow as well. "Please," he added. "He'll just use it against you."

"Grace couldn't have killed him," Cara argued. "I was with her. We were here working."

"You worked all night?" Gibbons asked smugly.

Cara didn't hesitate. "I've worked overnight on projects with Grace numerous times. Yes, I was here. She never left her room that night."

"You do understand, Ms. Gunter," Gibbons cautioned, "that perjury carries a very stiff penalty."

She put an arm around Grace's shoulders. "It's the truth."

Judging by the shock Grace hadn't quite been able to conceal from her expression, Rob wasn't buying it. He understood Cara wanted to help, but she was likely only making things worse.

Gibbons chuckled as if he too saw right through the ruse. "We'll see, ladies. Maybe the two of you worked together that night. The question is, did your joint efforts result in murder?"

Chapter Twelve

It was almost midnight.

Grace paced the parlor in her private quarters. Thank God Liam was asleep.

What the hell was she going to do?

She hugged herself, rubbed her arms in hopes of warding off the chill that was coming from deep inside.

Adam was dead. Some part of her considered that she should be at least a little sad because he was Liam's father. But it was difficult to feel anything other than relief when put into perspective with who and what he had been. A killer. One who'd murdered at least four women. Why would she feel anything for his loss?

The world was a better place without him.

And what about Joe Pierce? He—a guest—had been murdered on her property. She closed her eyes and rode out the new wave of defeat. She wasn't sure the inn could survive all that was no doubt coming. The media would flock to the inn like buzzards to roadkill as soon as the news was out. The world would learn the truth about who she was and her troubled past.

No one in this little community would look at her the same. She would never be trusted again. And how could she blame them? She had basically lied by omission to every person she'd come to know since her arrival. Not one person had known the truth about her and Liam.

Now she would have to face the repercussions of that somewhat self-serving decision. Protecting Liam had been her primary concern, but she couldn't deny wanting to protect herself as well.

Diane, Cara, the Wilborns—they had all believed in her, trusted her.

Grace slowed in her pacing. Cara had lied to protect her. She and Grace hadn't had the opportunity to talk privately since the unexpected announcement. The CSI team had arrived and then the medical examiner's van. This end of Mockingbird Lane was lit up like a Christmas scene from a horror movie. She had been exiled to her quarters. Diane and Cara were ordered to separate rooms in which they would be staying until this was sorted out.

Her fingers went to her lips to stop the trembling there. Where had the knife come from? The only thing she had put under the sink was the locket she'd found on the porch. But instead of finding a locket, Gibbons had found a knife. The same one that may have been used on Adam and possibly Mr. Pierce. Grace didn't have to wonder if that would be the case. Of course it would be. The knife wouldn't have been under her sink otherwise.

How did this happen? Who had taken the locket?

Whoever did this, it wasn't her. She could not have killed anyone.

Her fingers formed a fist and she pressed it hard against her lips to hold back the scream building in her throat.

Rob was still standing by her. Nothing Gibbons had thrown on the table had seemed to give him pause. Grace was very thankful for his loyalty, but she didn't deserve it. She had lied to him as well.

How foolish she had been to think that perhaps in time they might be able to have some kind of relationship beyond friendship.

"So much for that," she grumbled under her breath. She paused at the window and stared out over the backyard. The entire area was lit up like an airport runway. Sergeant Snelling's team of forensic investigators was swarming every inch of the property. Spotlights had been brought into the shed and placed around the yard in strategic places. Beyond all that was the sheer darkness that spanned out over the cliff. There were no stars to see tonight. The sky was a blanket of black with a mere sliver of a moon barely visible.

Her chest tightened with the loss she understood was coming. Loss of business for certain and loss of friendships no doubt.

She supposed she could sell the place and take Liam somewhere new to start over again. But it would be more difficult this time. He wasn't an infant anymore. He would be sad…and so would she.

A soft rap on the door had her hurrying in that direction. She hoped it was Rob and that there was news of who had done this latest awful thing.

She swung the door open, but it wasn't Rob.

"Cara." Grace glanced beyond her. "Gibbons won't be happy if he finds us talking."

Cara walked in, causing Grace to step back. She quickly closed the door, then hurried to the window and closed the shutters. Cara wandered to the fireplace, stood there staring into the flames.

Grace joined her, feeling a sudden need for a glass of something strong. She rarely drank alcohol at all, but if there was ever a time, this was it.

"Why did you lie to Gibbons about our being together?" she asked her friend.

Cara looked taken aback. "Lie?" She shook her head. "I didn't lie. Don't you remember? You called me right after the police left. You were so upset about someone coming onto the porch. You were horrified that Liam had gotten up without you knowing it and saw the person."

No. Grace wouldn't have forgotten that…

"Oh." She nodded. "Of course. I—I remember."
Liar.

"We sat right here for hours. Had some sherry. You were so upset." Cara shook her head again. "I felt so bad for you. You finally fell asleep on the sofa about two thirty and I left."

Grace's heart sank to her feet. Cara must be right.

She had fallen asleep on the sofa. Cara couldn't have known that if she hadn't been here. "You shouldn't worry so much about us, but I do appreciate being able to count on you at even the worst of times."

Cara put an arm around her shoulders. "We're family. And I meant what I said about Liam. If you want me to take care of him at my grandmother's cabin until this is finished, you know I would be happy to do so."

Maybe she should have taken Cara up on this offer already. How selfish to want to keep her child close with all that was going on.

"You're right. I'll talk to Rob and Gibbons and see if the two of you can leave in the morning. Liam doesn't need to be here with all this."

How did she protect her child from the rising insanity? From her own dance on the edge of reality?

Send him away from it. It was the only logical step.

"Sounds good." Cara hugged her. "Would you like me to prepare some hot chocolate for you? You might sleep better. Or I could pour us some sherry. We'd both sleep well then."

"Thanks, but it's late. You go on. I'll be fine."

Another knock at the door drew both Grace's and Cara's attention there. They stared at each other for a moment, and then Grace hurried to the door. She hoped no other bodies had been discovered.

It was a miracle both remaining guests hadn't requested to check out already.

Grace opened the door to Diane, who stood there clad in her pajamas and wringing her hands.

"I couldn't sleep. I saw the light under your door and figured you couldn't either."

Grace opened the door wider. "That seems to be the trend tonight."

Diane came in and Grace closed the door.

Cara waved. "Same here."

Diane hugged her arms around herself and joined Cara at the fire. "What a mess."

Grace wandered to the double windows that overlooked the backyard. She cracked open the shutter just enough to see. "Maybe we'll hear soon what they've found out there." Besides Pierce's body, she kept to herself.

"I'm still reeling," Diane confessed. "I mean, I hated Joe for what he did. Frankly, I never expected to see him again. But to have him murdered—right here where I work—it's beyond bizarre."

"I get that," Grace admitted. She left the window and joined the others in front of the flames. She stretched out her hands, feeling chilled to the bone. "I thought Adam was going to prison for the rest of his life. I never thought I'd have to see him again or have him invade my life."

"How—" Cara snapped her mouth shut as if she'd thought better of what she'd intended to ask.

"What?" Grace searched her face.

"It's nothing," Cara assured her.

Grace hated that she felt annoyed by her friend's response, but she did. Maybe only because she was on the edge already. "Ask whatever's on your mind. Please."

Cara searched her face for a moment. "You never noticed anything off about him? Nothing that made you the least bit uneasy?"

Grace had gotten that question before. So many times. She stared into the flames. "I wish I had. But the truth is, he seemed perfectly normal. He was funny, charming, thoughtful. I know it sounds crazy, but he acted as if he really wanted to take care of me. Especially after he found out about the baby. It was like he'd been waiting for that moment his whole life. He fussed over me continuously."

She couldn't say more. The words she'd said already had her insides wrenched too tight. She wished none of it were true. She wished she had never felt anything at all for him. That she'd never known him…but then she wouldn't have Liam.

How did one put that in perspective and voice it to another person?

"You didn't know," Diane said. "My situation was nothing on the caliber of yours, but I believed in Joe. I trusted him completely. I had no idea he would go so far to get the story. It was like nothing else mattered, especially not another person's life or my feelings." She looked to Cara. "Have you ever had anyone betray you that way?"

Cara laughed. "Only once. But then, once is enough, isn't it?"

"More than enough," Grace agreed.

"So true," Diane murmured.

"You two should get some sleep," Grace suggested, feeling the need to be alone. She was confident she wouldn't sleep, but she needed to think. To figure out where she went from here.

Diane hugged her. "See you in the morning."

Grace hugged her back, then did the same with Cara. "Thanks." She drew back, looked from one to the other. "Both of you. This would have been far harder without you."

When Grace had closed the door behind them, she checked on Liam. He'd insisted on sleeping in his own bed tonight. She sat down on the edge and brushed the hair from his eyes. How she loved this child. She hoped so hard that she could keep him safe and somehow protect him in the future from this nightmare.

She kissed his cheek and turned out the light on his bedside table. She wandered back to the parlor and stared out the window at the scene taking place. Maybe it would be better if she checked her guests out in the morning and closed down the inn for a while.

She wasn't so sure the inn would survive anyway, so what was a few bad reviews for sending guests away? No doubt both her current guests would be posting about the murder, and she didn't blame them.

She crossed her arms over her chest and thought about how she couldn't remember calling Cara on Sunday night after the police had gone. Why couldn't she remember something so important? Forgetting about registering a guest and misplacing her keys weren't such huge deals. But to forget calling over a friend after the police had searched your property for a would-be intruder?

Who was she kidding? It had happened before. However, she wanted to rationalize it or doubt she would have made such a mistake. She had.

This was real and it was happening. Again.

Grace reminded herself of all that she'd learned the last go-round. This would pass. She would make it through to the other side.

As long as whoever had murdered Adam and Joe Pierce was found and stopped.

She searched her memories for any discussion of associates Adam had before. Any friends who had visited their home. But there was no one. She and Adam never went out with other couples. He never had friends over. He rarely talked about work or his past. He had no family—at least, that was what he'd claimed. He'd told her his parents died when he was a baby and he'd been adopted. His adopted parents were older and had no other children. They had died when he was in college. To Grace's knowledge, there was no one else in Adam's life, and she felt sure Gibbons would have mentioned if he had discovered any differently.

For months after his arrest and before her breakdown, she had followed the investigation very closely. Gibbons had checked in with her at least weekly. There had been no contacts or connections to Adam found. His employer only knew what Adam presented to him. Hard worker. Top earner. He had been friendly and charming to everyone on a very superficial level. No friendships. No hanging out. No luncheons. He only attended the work functions required of him.

And he was the only employee who took two vacations at precise intervals without exception. He requested those days off every year. Though he'd been with the company for four years when he and Grace met, none of his coworkers knew anything at all about his life. Only his wife's name. Not that they were expecting a child or anything else.

Why had he kept secret the fact that he was going to be a father?

Their whole life together had been one lie after the other, all built on a make-believe existence.

A knock on the door had her turning toward it. Had Diane or Cara decided to come back? Was one of the guests leaving now for fear that he would be the next victim?

Grace pushed the awful thoughts away and went to the door. She drew in a big breath and opened it.

Rob.

The fatigue and worry on his face, in the set of his shoulders, had her pulse racing with a new rush of adrenaline.

"Please tell me nothing else has happened."

He stepped in, prompting her to step back. He closed the door, then gestured to the sofa. "Let's sit and go over what we know so far."

She nodded, unable to find her voice to respond. Grace made her way to the sofa and sat. She reminded herself to breathe while Rob took the seat across from her. Her hands wrung together. This was the nightmare that didn't want to end. She didn't see how things could get worse, but deep inside she understood they could. Much worse.

"Your prints were found in the shed," Rob said, finally. "But that was to be expected since you live here and it's your shed."

She nodded, knowing that was just the easy part. "What about the knife?"

"Your prints were on the knife handle too."

She wanted to rant, to get up and stamp her feet. She had not touched that knife. It took every ounce of restraint she possessed to remain seated. "I didn't put that knife under the sink. I have never seen that knife before."

"I know. Snelling is working on that. He believes the prints at the Cashion crime scene were planted. He's getting confirmation on that. It'll be tomorrow sometime before he can make an official confirmation. He believes the ones on the knife will be forged as well."

Relief swam through her veins. "Thank God."

"Grace." Rob braced his elbows on his knees, his hands clasped between them. "We know you didn't do this. It's important that you understand this."

She managed a bumpy nod. "I hope so."

"You don't have to hope. It's a fact. No one believes you did this. Not even Gibbons. He just has to be sure before he admits as much."

"I'm not surprised. He was the same way before. Determined to prove I knew something I didn't."

"I think," Rob said, "giving him maybe more credit than he deserves at this point, that what he's really trying to do is prove you don't know anything. His methods leave something to be desired, but he's worked some pretty nasty cases. Stuff like that changes a guy."

She supposed she could understand how that would happen. She nodded. "Thank you for telling me. I'll keep that in mind going forward." She stared at her hands, wished she didn't have to share the next part. But Rob had been too kind and helpful to her for her to leave him in the dark. "Cara said that I called her over that night—Sunday—after the police left. She says she stayed with me for several hours, which is why she told Gibbons I couldn't have killed Adam."

Rob nodded, waited for her to go on.

"I thought she was lying for me. I don't remember calling her or her being here."

Rob rubbed a hand over his shadowed jaw. "Does she have any proof that you called her? Do you have any that you didn't?"

She straightened, a thought occurring to her. "I can check my cell." She dug it from her pocket and scanned the recent calls. There were no calls beyond today's. She frowned. "Apparently I cleared my call log."

"Do you remember clearing it?" he asked gently.

She shook her head. "I don't." She exhaled a big

breath and went for broke. It was time she came completely clean with this too-kind man. "What I do remember is putting a locket in a plastic bag and hiding it under the sink because I was terrified. My picture was inside. That's what I found on the porch after Adam was here. I didn't tell anyone because I was afraid. Now, what? Forty-eight hours later there's no locket but there is a knife? A bloody knife with my prints on it."

"You didn't tell me," he pointed out, his voice soft, gentle. Not accusing or angry as she would have expected—as she deserved.

"I was in denial. I didn't want it to be true and I thought maybe if I…" She shook her head. "I don't know what I thought. Apparently, I don't even know what I actually did."

"Have you considered that someone wants you to feel as if you're losing your mind? To doubt yourself?"

She searched his face, not daring to say how desperately she wanted that to be true. "But how could Adam or his follower know about my breakdown? No one knew. I was with Val and then I came here after. I've never discussed it with anyone until I told you."

"Have you been in contact with the woman—this Val?"

"No. She said we should never have contact of any kind. To prevent anyone from using her to find me."

"Smart lady." He took a breath. "We should have Gibbons request a welfare check. Maybe have a detective in the area interview her. See if she's been visited by anyone asking questions. She's older. She may have inadvertently mentioned you."

He was right. Val would be seventy-five or eighty. She could be in a nursing home by now with dementia. Grace had no idea.

"All right."

"My advice at this point," he said, "would be for you and Liam to go someplace safe until this is done. Cara and Diane can take care of things here. I've called Sheriff Norwood, and she's sending me four additional deputies. One will be here at the inn at all times."

She had been thinking the same thing. "Cara offered her grandmother's cabin. She said she'd take Liam there and keep him hidden until this was over."

"Gibbons wants you to stay here as a lure to whoever is behind all this. He hasn't said this, but I'm beginning to see how his mind works."

Grace shook her head. "If I have no choice, I can stay, but not Liam. I want him away from this."

"You do have a choice," Rob said. "This is my jurisdiction and I have the final say. I'm taking you and Liam to my cabin, and I'm staying with you until Gibbons and Reynolds find whoever is acting on Locke's behalf or whatever the hell he's doing."

She held his gaze. "Are you going with us because that's likely the only way Gibbons will allow us to leave?"

Rob held her gaze for a long moment. "I'm going because I'm not letting you or Liam out of my sight until I know it's safe."

Grace wanted to feel good about his words, but

it was impossible, all things considered. "We might never be safe."

He managed a sad smile. "Then I guess it's a good thing I don't have a problem with however long it takes."

The warmth his words elicited almost chased away the cold leaching into her bones. Almost.

The one thing that prevented her from feeling happy about his words was the idea that Adam Locke had destroyed everything she'd loved once before. Though he was dead now, apparently that wasn't going to stop him from doing it again.

Chapter Thirteen

Wednesday, February 21, 8:00 a.m.

Rob walked the perimeter of the property. Things were quiet now save the half-dozen news vans parked along Mockingbird Lane. Anytime now they would gather around the gate and start watching for some sign of Grace or anyone else who might provide a sound bite. Rob had given a statement. He'd simply said there had been two murders. The perpetrator remained unknown, and folks should be on the lookout for anything at all out of the ordinary. They should lock their doors and check on shut-ins. Vigilance was required until they had this case under control.

About two this morning the ME had taken Pierce's body to the morgue. His next of kin, a younger brother, had been notified. The CSI folks had finished up by four and packed it in. Rob had sent Reynolds home for some sleep. Two of the deputies Norwood had sent were on scene, one stationed out front, one in back. After lunch Reynolds would be back. Rob wanted him here at the inn once he left with Grace and Liam.

Reynolds would be his eyes and ears until it was safe for Rob to bring them back.

First thing this morning he'd told Grace they would be leaving shortly after noon. The next few hours should give her plenty of time to prepare for leaving the inn with Cara and Diane in charge. One of his deputies was stopping in to check on the Wilborns this morning. Grace was worried. She hadn't heard from the couple since early on Tuesday. She had a right to be worried with one of her guests dead and her ex trekking all the way here only to end up murdered.

Rob hoped Grace had managed at least a couple of hours of sleep last night—this morning, actually. He couldn't deny being concerned about the things she appeared to have forgotten, but he also recognized there was room for someone else to be behind the problems. It was too soon to make a call one way or the other, but his money was on Grace being gaslighted, particularly if someone knew about Grace's past breakdown. Gibbons had a detective friend in the Lake Tahoe area who would be paying a visit to Valentina Hicks this morning. If she'd spoken to anyone about Grace lately, that might provide a lead. At this point, Rob would take anything.

There had already been two bodies. He didn't want to uncover any more.

He'd asked Reynolds if he'd noted Cara's arrival at the inn after the search on Sunday night, but the deputy hadn't seen her. He had driven around the block a couple of times, so it was possible Cara had arrived during one of those occasions. With her compact car, she could easily have parked it near the garage and Reynolds hadn't noticed.

Rob stepped onto the terrace that ran across the back of the inn and knocked on the back door. He wanted all doors kept locked until further notice. An assistant who worked in the sheriff's office was running a background check on the remaining guests, Russell Ames and Henry Brower, as well as Diane and Cara. Since he'd already done a preliminary check on the two women, the new look was a deeper dig. Cara Gunter had roots here. Her grandmother was a lifelong resident. Rob had interviewed both women personally, but it never hurt to ask around town. Information was power. The lack of information was the road to defeat.

The turn of the locks and then the door opening brought him face-to-face with Diane. "I have a fresh pot of coffee brewed," she said. "Breakfast is on the sideboard in the dining room. Detective Gibbons is already in there."

Gibbons had turned in around four thirty. Rob doubted the man had gotten any more sleep than he had. Sleeping when there was a killer breathing down their necks was not easy.

"Thanks, Diane."

Liam sat on a stool at the island. He held up a slice of bacon. "Eat!"

Rob grinned. "Looks yummy, buddy."

When Grace walked in, she tried to smile and failed. "Did you talk to the reporters?"

He nodded. "I did. But they'll try to talk to you or

anyone else who shows her or his face outside, so keep that in mind."

"They'll follow us when we leave," she said, obviously weary.

"They would, but I have a plan for that."

"Good. Okay." She smiled at her son. "As soon as Liam is finished up, we'll go get packed up."

"Woad twip!" Liam grinned and reached for a biscuit.

Rob smiled. "That's right, buddy. We're taking a road trip."

He poured himself a fresh mug of coffee and headed for the dining room to catch up with Gibbons.

The older detective was just finishing his breakfast when Rob joined him at the table. The two guests were finished already and moving toward the lobby.

"My deputy," Rob said, slowing their departure, "will see that the reporters don't give you any trouble."

Both men nodded. Neither looked excited about the idea of wading through a flock of reporters.

"You talked to the press already?" Gibbons asked as Rob picked up a plate from the buffet.

"I did." He gave him the details as he filled his plate. "After lunch I'll move Grace and Liam."

"I had some reservations about that," Gibbons admitted, "but after the phone call I just received, I'm more convinced than ever that whoever is behind this is here for Grace and her son."

Rob's instincts alerted. "Did you hear from your friend in Lake Tahoe?"

Gibbons gave a nod. "He's retired, so he spends a lot of time fishing. Gets out early to beat the crowds, so he popped in at the Hicks place before sunrise this morning. He's got the local authorities there now."

Oh, hell. "The old woman's dead?"

Gibbons nodded. "House was ransacked. Whoever killed her was looking for information. We both know it was for anything that could be found on Grace."

Damn, he hated to give this news to Grace. "I don't suppose he left us any clues."

Gibbons shrugged. "Too soon to tell, but there is one kicker."

Rob's gaze narrowed. "That is…?"

"Hicks has been dead for at least a year. That's based on her calendar being open to February and the expiration date on the milk container in her fridge. My friend is no medical examiner, but he's guessing, based on the condition of the body, that the time frame is reasonably accurate."

"So our killer has been putting this plan together for a long time." Damn. No wonder he'd left no evidence except what he wanted them to find.

"Looks that way." Gibbons pushed his plate away. "If he's had that much time, then he has the lay of the land here. He could be living here, for all we know. Maybe knows who is who in the community. You should watch out, Vaughn. If that's the case, he likely knows you have a personal interest in his target."

Rob pushed his plate away as well. He'd lost his appetite. "I'll be watching," Rob promised. "I won't go down so easy."

Gibbons nodded. "I'm guessing he's figured that out already too."

"Do you know how long you'll be gone?"

Grace considered Diane's question. "Not long, I hope. The sooner this is over, the better." She finger-combed her son's hair. "Every minute that we live like this terrifies me."

"I can't even begin to imagine." Diane visibly shivered.

"Can't imagine what?" Cara pushed through the swinging door, a load of plates in her hands.

"Deputy Vaughn is moving Liam and me to a safe house until they find the source of the trouble."

For a moment Cara looked surprised.

"It's the only way Gibbons would agree to our leaving," Grace explained quickly in hopes of assuaging any offense Cara might take about Grace not accepting her offer.

Cara nodded knowingly. "I think that's the best plan." She winked at Diane. "Does this mean you and I are in charge?"

Diane grinned. "We are."

"Will we have any security?" Cara asked, opening the dishwasher.

"Deputy Reynolds and at least one other deputy will be here with you."

Cara made an agreeable sound. "Okay, I can live with that."

Diane moved to Grace and put an arm around her shoulders. "We will take very good care of everything until you're back."

"It's about time you took a vacation," Cara chimed in. "You work too hard."

"'Cation!" Liam said triumphantly.

Grace relaxed a little. "For a little while," she promised her son.

Now that she thought about it, she and Liam had never been on a vacation. When this was over, she intended to remedy that sad condition.

She helped Cara and Diane clean up the kitchen and dining room before heading to the registration desk to take care of a few things there. Cara took Liam to their quarters to play. Liam adored Cara. He'd loved the inn's former assistant too. Kendall's death was such a shame.

Grace scrolled through her calendar. So far, nothing she hadn't expected had occurred this morning. She certainly hoped things stayed that way. The next guests arrived on Friday, three couples. She'd called Mr. Warren and asked if they could postpone the exterior work until later in the spring. He'd been surprisingly agreeable in this conversation. Grace supposed he'd heard about the murders. Who wanted to send a crew of workers to a crime scene?

Grace made a few more calls before walking through the inn for a final look around. She didn't dare go outside for fear of running into a reporter. Upstairs, she walked from room to room. Checked the unoccupied ones, mostly so she could look out the windows and see what sort of crowd had gathered.

The half-dozen news vans Rob had mentioned earlier had been joined by four others. Mostly statewide channels. Nothing national yet. But they would come. The Sweetheart Killer murders hadn't gone unnoticed by the big networks. Adam's demise wouldn't go uncovered either.

As she walked back down the long, carpeted hall, she paused outside Mr. Ames's door. She still couldn't understand how she had made his reservation and not remembered. Like Pierce, he didn't look familiar to her. In fact, he'd mostly ignored her since his arrival. He had given her a look this morning after all the excitement of last night. But who wouldn't?

Grace moved on. She descended the stairs and went to the reading parlor. This room was one of her favorite places. Mostly because of the wall of shelves loaded with books. There was also a well-stocked bar.

She walked back into the hall, checked the powder room under the stairs. She'd have to remind Cara to see that it was cleaned. She had no idea how long it would be before the Wilborns could return to work. All the common areas would need a good cleaning before Friday.

Grace took a long, deep breath. It felt good to think about something besides murder and mayhem.

She strolled through the dining room, checked the pastry trays. Her bear claws had gone over well with their guests. Focusing on her baking this morning had helped take her mind off the horror of last night.

Her father had told her many times growing up how much her mother had loved to bake. Sometimes when he would tell her stories of her mother, Grace had almost been able to smell the delicious scents his words conjured. Perhaps the smells were memories. Either way, Grace had loved listening to him talk about her mother. He would say a man could only love one woman the way he had loved her mother.

Grace didn't even bother wondering anymore if she would ever know a love like that. Her mind instantly summoned up the image of Rob. She didn't doubt that he was the sort of man who could make that kind of love happen. He liked her. She knew he did. But considering all that had happened the past few days, he might not want to take that risk with her, and she wouldn't blame him.

She sighed. This was the worst possible time for her mind to be wandering in that direction. She went to the lobby, checked out the windows and groaned at the growing crowd of reporters and what she suspected were curious residents.

Grace felt sad that the life she'd built here was now over. Wherever things went from here, they wouldn't be the same.

Depressed all over again, she checked the kitchen. Empty. Maybe Diane had joined Cara and Liam. With her work done, there was no reason not to.

Grace made her way to their private quarters. Diane and Liam were sitting on the floor watching his favorite cartoon.

"I'm just going to pack a few things so Liam and I are ready when it's time to go."

Diane nodded. "Let me know if you need any help. Cara popped out to check on her grandmother since we may be here for a few days."

"That was a good idea." Grace felt bad for keeping her away from her grandmother. She hoped Cara had a friend who could check in on the elderly woman.

In the bedroom, Grace picked through her closet until she found the overnight bag she'd used when she fled California. She'd taken nothing but what she could fit into that small bag. This was much the same situation. She grabbed a few items, then went to Liam's room and packed his little backpack with clothes and his favorite stuffed animal.

After putting the two bags by the parlor door, she made her way to the lobby. The inn's landline rang, and she hurried to the desk to answer it. "Lookout Inn."

"Hi, Gia."

Grace froze. The voice was female. No one she recognized.

"If you walk back to the fireplace and look out the window on the right, you'll see me."

Grace walked to the window and stared out. A woman with red hair and dressed in a white parka waved to her with her free hand. Her other hand held the cell phone to her ear.

"Who is this?" Grace didn't recognize the woman. Not from this distance, anyway.

"This is Renae Keller from the *Bay Area News*. I'm sure you'll remember me if you think about it."

The name and face jogged no memories for Grace. The truth was, there had been so many back then, she only remembered the most cutthroat of the bunch. Evidently, this one hadn't risen to that level—or perhaps hadn't sunk to that level.

Grace's heart thudded with frustration and no small amount of anger. "What do you want?" She almost laughed at herself. The woman was a reporter. She wanted whatever she could get.

"Did you murder your ex-husband? Not that anyone would blame you if you did. In fact, you would be considered a hero by most."

Grace ended the call.

The reporter stared at her as she reached up and closed the window shutters. The phone in her hand rang again.

Grace realized this was the way it would be. The phone would ring constantly. She turned off the handset and returned it to its cradle. Then she walked around the downstairs area and closed the shutters on all the windows. She turned off the ringer on the other two handsets.

The back door opened and she froze, hoping it wouldn't be a reporter who had sneaked past the deputies serving as security.

She saw Rob and sighed with relief.

Thank goodness.

"Everything okay in here?" he asked, searching her face as if he noted the discomfort she felt.

"Fine." She produced what she hoped passed for

a smile. "We're packed and ready to go whenever you are."

"We checked in with the Wilborns. They both officially have the flu, but they're doing pretty well and hope to be back to work sometime next week."

"That's a relief." At this point, Grace was worried about everyone close to her.

"Deputy Reynolds will be in charge of things here. He'll keep me posted at regular intervals, so you don't have to worry about anything once we're gone."

"Thank you. I worry about Diane and Cara being here, but I really do appreciate not having to shut down the inn entirely."

"They'll be in good hands and so will you and Liam."

Her smile was real this time. "Thank you."

Grace didn't see any reason to tell him about the reporter's call. She should have known they would start calling the inn's official phone number. If they had her cell number, it would be blowing up.

"We're moving back the reporters to the other end of the lane. As soon as they are blocked in, we'll go. I don't want to risk one following us. So be prepared. When Reynolds gives the word, we're out of here."

"We'll be ready."

Grace hurried back to her quarters. "We'll be leaving soon," she told Diane. Then to her little boy she said, "Liam, we should be prepared to go. Deputy Rob will be ready to take us on our adventure soon."

"I ready!" He executed an air punch for emphasis. Grace loved that he was excited. She went to her room and found her favorite hiking boots and tugged them on. She found Liam's and helped him into them.

"We'll put on our coats when we're ready to go, okay?"

Liam nodded at her, his little smile melting her heart.

"I'll call you if anything comes up," Diane promised. "I don't want you to worry. Cara and I will take care of everything the same way you would."

"I know you will. Just stay inside and stay safe. If anything at all feels wrong, get Deputy Reynolds on it ASAP. Don't hesitate."

Diane gave her a salute. "Yes, ma'am."

The door opened and Rob poked his head in. "Time to go."

Grace picked up Liam and said goodbye to her friend.

She told herself again that this was the right thing to do.

The only thing to do.

Chapter Fourteen

Chestnut Bridge Hollow, 2.30 p.m.

Rob's getaway was only twenty miles from the inn, but it seemed much farther considering the place was so far off the beaten path. This was where he spent his off time, he'd explained. The historic log cabin had been in his family for four generations. The part he hadn't mentioned was that the cabin sat on hundreds of acres that flowed right up to the Tennessee River. The driveway from the main road wound more than a mile into the woods before reaching the clearing where the cabin, a big old white barn and several sheds spread across acres of grass and enormous old trees. Beyond that were the majestic woods that went on seemingly forever, rising up the mountains all around.

It was perfect…incredibly picturesque.

The memory of all those reporters rushing toward his SUV had her even more grateful for this getaway. It would have been only a matter of time before one or more would have figured out a way to get into the inn. She so appreciated Rob bringing them here and was grateful that he'd made double sure they weren't followed.

"No wonder you love coming here," Grace said, the view taking her breath away. As much as she loved the mountaintop views from the inn, this was truly magnificent in its own right. But more important, it wasn't easy to find.

Rob was right. She and Liam would be safe here.

Grace relaxed for the first time in days.

Rob parked his SUV and shut off the engine. "This is the first time I've brought anyone here with me since…last year."

She understood. "I'm sorry it had to be under current circumstances." She hoped it wasn't a terrible inconvenience. She hated the idea of being such a bother. She'd brought him nothing but trouble lately.

"I'm glad you're here no matter the circumstances." He smiled and she relaxed again.

"Thank you."

"No thanks necessary." He climbed out and opened the back door. "Come on, buddy." Rob released Liam from his car seat. "There's something I want to show you."

He set Liam on the ground and grabbed their bags.

Grace followed the two toward the cabin. Liam, who insisted on carrying his backpack, kept pointing at different things—like the barn—and asking what was inside. She suspected he hoped for horses or cows. Maybe pigs.

"There are two horses," Rob explained. "They're

in the pasture, so they may be down at the stream right now. We'll track them down later and maybe your mom will let me take you for a ride sometime."

Liam jumped up and down and shouted, "Please! Please! Please!"

Rob paused at the front door of the gorgeous cabin to unlock it. "Sorry, Grace. I should have asked you first."

"I think it's a great idea," she said, letting him off the hook. To her son, she offered, "How about we see how the weather is tomorrow? We should get settled now and rest up. How about it?"

"'Kay!" Excitement danced across his little face.

Inside was every bit as breathtaking as outside. When Rob had called the place a cabin, she'd anticipated three or four rooms. Rustic. It was a log cabin, all right, but this was huge. When they entered, what had likely once been the main room had been turned into a massive foyer with views straight through to a wall of windows that looked out over the river. Grace walked in that direction. A large addition had been built onto the back of the original cabin that included soaring vaulted ceilings cloaked in natural wood and windows that extended from the floor to that peak and provided incredible views all around.

"Wow."

"I added this part when my mom insisted on turning the place over to me. She said she wasn't interested in spending much time out here once Dad was gone. My sister is too busy with her career in Nashville to get out this way often. She preferred the beach house in Florida my parents thought they couldn't live without when they retired. Turned out my sister was the only one who really liked it."

Grace stood at the window staring at the river. It was so close, almost overpowering and at the same time alluring. "I don't know how you ever leave this place."

"Work." He grinned, ruffled Liam's curly hair. Her son too was enthralled with the river view. "A man's gotta earn his keep."

Grace surveyed the room again. "I can just imagine how beautiful this place is at Christmas."

"Last year was the first time I'd put up a tree since my dad died. It didn't feel right, and then the renovation was going on. But this last time I went all out. It was great." He shrugged. "A little much for just me, but I enjoyed it. I invited a couple of my friends and their families over. It was fun."

How on earth was this man still single? Then she remembered him telling her about his former fiancée. Grace was certain the woman was a fool. But then, the heart knew what the heart wanted. Sometimes it made no sense to anyone else. Grace understood this better than most. No one could understand how she'd fallen in love with a monster. A killer. A liar. But she hadn't seen that side of him. Emotion had blinded her, she supposed.

"Let me show you around." Rob turned back to the older part of the house. "The kitchen is this way."

The newly remodeled kitchen took up most of the right side of the house. Whatever had been upstairs had been removed to make room for another soaring ceiling. It was modern and at the same time very country. Grace was impressed with his remodeling decisions.

"You did a great job." The dining area had a huge bay window facing that river view.

"My mother was impressed, but I can't claim all the credit. Most of the design decisions were based on input from my sister. She also wrangled me some killer discounts."

Grace was glad for that. She'd been certain he was going to say the decisions had been made by his former fiancée, which left whoever he was involved with in the future to live in her design.

Though, admittedly, it was a really good one either way.

Back at the other end of the original part of the house was a powder room, an owner's suite and the staircase that led to the three bedrooms upstairs. All had been updated. All were impressively well done. If the place was hers, Grace wouldn't change a thing.

When the tour was over, Rob carried Grace's bag to the owner's suite. "You and Liam can have this room. I'll take the sofa where I can keep an eye on all the access points."

Grace started to argue but his reasoning was sound. He needed to be able to keep eyes on the doors. She was grateful for his vigilance.

Liam followed Rob back into the main room. The boy adored having Rob around. Grace had noticed this a couple of months ago. Every time Rob would drop by the inn for a meal or just to check on them, Liam was drawn to him. He was otherwise fairly shy with anyone outside their close circle. But not with Rob.

Grace had wrestled with the urge to make more of Rob's interest than there was. But then a part of her had given in and started looking forward to his calls and occasional visits.

She sighed and opened her bag. Probably not smart to make too much of this either. He was trying to protect them. This was not a romantic getaway.

A chill made her shiver. Was it just her or was this room colder than the others? She walked around the room, checked the windows. All secure. Then she moved on to the attached bath and saw the problem. The window over the claw-foot tub was open just a couple of inches. It was a large window, so even that little gap allowed the crisp winter air to slip in. She glanced around the room and over the ceiling and didn't spot an exhaust fan, which likely explained the window being open a bit. Although the claw-foot tub and the pedestal-style vanity were original looking, she'd wager the large shower was not. She imagined some seriously steamy air would come from the shower.

Before she could stop it, her mind conjured the image of Rob in that shower, the water slipping over his naked body. Steam rising around him.

"And that's about enough of that," she grumbled as she climbed into the tub and closed the window.

When she made her way back to the main room,

Rob and Liam were on the deck, seated in two of the rocking chairs. Her heart squeezed. She so much wanted a happy life for her son. She wondered if she would ever be able to make that happen. She had thought she'd been mostly successful until Sunday night.

How had she ever believed for one minute she would be free of that monster as long as he was still breathing?

Even now that Adam was dead she had to worry about this partner or followers. Until now she hadn't allowed herself to consider what this person—the person who'd killed Adam and Pierce—wanted. Certainly he wasn't there to protect her and Liam.

The thing that terrified her more than any other thought was the idea that he wanted Liam—not just Grace or maybe not even Grace. Every instinct she possessed was screaming that this killer wanted Liam above all else. Either to hurt him or simply to have him. It was feasible this person who was clearly obsessed with Adam would be obsessed with this child. Maybe Adam had seen this too and attempted to be rid of him, and that person killed Adam.

Grace rolled her eyes. She refused to give Adam any benefit of the doubt. Whatever he had done or said that caused his death—assuming that was the case—it was not some heroic deed.

Her cell phone rang and Grace jumped. She pressed a hand to her chest and took a breath. Just thinking about Adam made her jumpy. She dug the phone from her pocket and smiled at the name on the screen.

Cara.

"Hey, was your grandmother okay?"

"She is," Cara said in her trademark perky tone. "I'm just calling to make sure you and Liam made it and to tell you that Diane and I have everything under control."

"We do!" Diane called out. The call was on speaker.

"Dinner is in the works, and surprisingly," Cara went on, "a good many of the reporters have peeled off. We're hoping they haven't tried to follow you to your secret destination."

Grace hoped not. "Several deputies blocked the end of the lane where they'd been pushed back to, so they couldn't get out until we were well on our way."

"Excellent," Diane said. "That Deputy Vaughn is pretty smart."

Grace wasn't getting into that conversation, even though her gaze was on the man at that very moment. She loved watching him with Liam.

"Any news from Detective Gibbons?"

"He and those CSI guys have been crawling all over the inn," Cara answered. "Mr. Brower has returned from his conference, but we haven't seen Mr. Ames since he left this morning. He may show up later. We're preparing for dinner as if he'll be here."

"Be sure to make plates for the deputies as well," Grace reminded her.

"Will do," Diane promised. "I'll even see that Detective Gibbons gets what he deserves."

"Oh, no," Grace said with a laugh. "That sounds ominous."

"Just kidding," Diane joked.

"What about the news?" Grace hadn't checked any headlines on her phone, and they hadn't turned on a television since their arrival here. She doubted she would be happy about the details already discovered about hers and Liam's lives.

"We shut the televisions off," Cara said. "We're living it. We don't need to see it."

Which meant it was bad. "Thanks, but you didn't answer my question."

"Told you," Diane muttered to Cara.

"Fine. If you must know, they're speculating you killed him—Locke, I mean," Cara said. "Pierce too."

Grace closed her eyes and waited a moment for the frustration to pass. She shouldn't be surprised. Of course they would say she was the killer. She had the most to gain with the bastard's death. It didn't matter that she didn't know Pierce. The media would make what they would of it all.

"The people who know and care about you won't believe what they suggest," Diane insisted. "You know they won't."

What Grace knew was that people believed what was shown to them over and over by the media. It had happened to her before, and it wouldn't be any different this time no matter how this played out.

"I appreciate the support," she said. "And I truly appreciate the two of you taking care of the inn until we're back. Watch out for each other."

"We always do," Diane said. "Be careful, Grace."

"Ditto," Cara chimed in.

Grace ended the call and decided to go to the kitchen to see what sort of supplies they had. Making dinner was the least she could do after all that Rob was doing for them.

The pantry was quite large. She wandered through, noted a good supply of dry and canned goods. Then she moved on to the refrigerator.

She checked the date on the carton of milk. It still had several days before expiring. There was a surprising array of fresh items. She could definitely work with this. She started to close the door, but something snagged her attention. She opened the door wider once more.

A thirty-two-ounce bottle of one of those sports drinks sat behind the milk and the orange juice. She reached toward it, noted that it was only half-full. So what? Lots of people drank sports drinks. No big deal.

Except this one had been Adam's favorite. This brand and this flavor. It was all he'd drunk besides the occasional beer or a glass of wine—both of which were rare. He'd insisted his body was a temple. He consumed very little sugar and never ever failed to have this sports drink in the refrigerator.

It was just a coincidence. It had to be.

Grace slammed the door shut.

It couldn't be anything else.

Except her instincts were screaming otherwise.

Rob stood, stretched. "Little man, we should get inside and see what your mom is up to."

"Can we see the horses?"

"We'll go out to the barn and have a look around in a little while. Maybe your mom will come with us."

"'Kay."

Rob opened the French door that led inside. Grace stood at the windows. She'd been watching them.

"I think Liam likes it here," Rob offered. Her expression was hard to read, but he suspected she was feeling unsettled. With all that was going on, she had every right.

She smiled, but it didn't reach her eyes. "It's a very peaceful place."

Liam tugged at his hand. "See the horses now?"

Rob smiled. "If it's okay with your mom, we'll go to the barn and call them in for a special treat."

Liam tugged at his mom now, repeating, "Please, please, please!"

"Sure. It'd be nice to get outside."

He should have thought of that. Grace and Liam had been cooped up in the inn since Sunday. No wonder the kid wanted outside so badly.

As they stepped off the porch, Rob pointed beyond the barn. "The land goes to the top of that mountain." He pointed in the other direction. "And just over the top in that direction. There are dozens of trails through the woods. As kids, my sister and I walked all over these woods."

"It's really beautiful." Grace surveyed the woods. Then she smiled. "I see the horses."

"I see!" Liam jumped up and down, trying to see what his mom saw.

Rob picked him up and sat him on his shoulders. "See beyond the barn? The horses are in their pasture. It goes all the way to the tree line at the base of the mountain. They have plenty of room for roaming and grazing and their own year-round stream for water."

When they reached the barn, Rob set Liam on his feet once more. "We'll go to the corral at the back of the barn and call them in. They know when I call for them that they're in for a special treat."

He showed Liam how to climb up on the rails of the fence so he could watch the horses gallop in. Grace stood next to him. She seemed as enthralled as her son. He was glad. She needed to relax. Rob called to Lucky and Dolly and their heads came up. They surveyed the scene for a moment, then started galloping toward the open corral. Once the horses entered the corral and settled down near the fence, he picked Liam up and showed him how to pet the animals so he didn't spook them. Then he helped Liam add their feed to two buckets, and the two of them gave the horses their special treat.

"They too big," Liam said, his eyes huge.

Rob laughed. "They are big but they're gentle. They won't try to hurt you. With a good horse, the only time you have to worry about being hurt is if you do something you shouldn't."

Liam peered up at him. "Not me. I a good boy."

Rob laughed. Grace did as well. It was good to hear her laugh.

After they'd fed the horses and petted them until Liam had grown bored, Rob gave his guests a mini tour. The woods marched right up to the pasture's edge and then to the clearing where the house and other outbuildings stood.

"That one," he said to Liam as he pointed to one of the oldest buildings on the property, "is the smoke-house."

Liam frowned. "Smoking house?"

"It's where folks used to cure their meat before there were refrigerators and freezers."

Liam pointed to another shed. "What's that one?"

"The chicken house."

"You gots chickens?" Liam looked intrigued.

"Sadly, I do not, but maybe one of these days when I'm here more often."

"Mom wants chickens."

Grace laughed. "How do you remember that?" She shook her head. "I don't even remember when, but I did say once that I would love a chicken coop and chickens. I'm just not sure the guests would appreciate them."

Liam stopped and looked around. "You gots dogs?"

Rob had expected that question. "I had a dog. Bandit. He was a really good dog and I had him for a very long time. He loved coming out here with me."

Liam's face fell. "Did he run away?"

"No, buddy, I'm sorry to say he just got too old and died. I buried him over there by that grove of oak trees." He pointed to the copse of trees that stood in the center of the driveway that circled the clearing. "Bandit used to lie there in the summer when it was hot. He could see everything happening around the house and barn from there."

Liam frowned. "You needa get another dog."

Rob smiled sadly. "I guess I do. Maybe you and I can go to the big animal shelter and find one to adopt."

"'Kay." Liam spotted the ancient swing set. "I wanna swing!"

He took off in that direction. Grace followed. "Be careful."

Rob caught up with her. "I'm sorry. I'm probably making way too many promises."

Grace shook her head. "I'm sure Liam would love all your suggestions." She winced as she watched her son scramble onto the lowest hanging swing.

"My married friends will tell you that I like spoiling kids."

She smiled then. "I can see that."

"Push me, Mommy!"

Grace gave Liam a small push. "Hang on tight."

Liam squealed with delight.

Grace gave him another gentle push. "Do you have friends over often?"

"No one since Christmas." Rob wished he had made the move to full-time living out here already. Soon, he hoped. He'd made a New Year's resolution to do that, but something always got in the way.

"I didn't think to suggest we stop at a market. I was glad to see there was milk in the fridge."

"Should be bottled water too." He made a face. "No soft drinks or juices. Sorry, I didn't think of that."

"Sports drinks are okay," she said.

"I've never cared for sports drinks. Mostly I stick with water or coffee. You?"

She flinched. "Water works for me."

He couldn't decide if the flinch was about something that had flown too near her face—nothing he'd seen—or something he'd said. Before he could ask, his cell vibrated. Rob pulled it from his pocket and checked the screen. *Reynolds.*

He flashed Grace a smile. "Excuse me."

He walked away from the swing as he accepted the call. "Hey, man, what's up?"

"Well, maybe nothing, but I can't seem to find Detective Gibbons."

Now, there was an update Rob hadn't been expecting. "Is his rental car there? I talked to him this morning."

"Yeah. That's the weird part. But I can't find him anywhere, and he is not answering his cell. I haven't heard from him since the two of you talked."

"Keep looking. Let me know the minute you find him." Rob ended the call and immediately put one through to Gibbons's cell number. The call went straight to voice mail.

Rob hoped like hell they didn't have another murder.

He glanced back at Grace and Liam. She was watching him. Was that suspicion he saw before she looked away? Seemed odd that she would be suspicious of him taking a call out of her earshot, but then if anyone had a right to be worried about every little thing, it was Grace.

The call from Reynolds had him worrying about the West Coast detective. Whatever had happened to Gibbons, the only thing Rob could do right now was protect Grace and Liam.

But if Gibbons was still breathing, where the hell would he be?

Had he taken a different vehicle and followed Rob here? Was he that hell-bent on keeping Grace and Liam in his sights?

Or maybe he was in this deeper than just as a detective. It was mighty damned convenient that he'd been able to get a flight from San Francisco to Chattanooga in such a timely manner.

What if Rob had been looking for the trouble in all the wrong places?

Chapter Fifteen

6:30 p.m.

Grace turned off the stove. Dinner was ready. She took the rolls out of the oven and set them on the stove top. There had been hamburger meat in the freezer, so she'd thawed it in the microwave and made a meat loaf. Instant potatoes and a can of green beans had to suffice as the sides. Not such a bad meal.

She set her hands on her hips and surveyed the room. As soon as Rob and Liam were in from seeing the horses, they could eat. Liam really enjoyed the time outside. As he got older, Grace had to make it a point to see that he had more of it.

Her cell chimed with a text, and she checked the screen. The number wasn't one in her contacts, but she recognized it. Detective Gibbons. Why was he contacting her? Rob had made it clear that the man was to go through him.

Grace rolled her eyes and opened the message.

This is Gibbons. You and Liam are not safe with Vaughn.

"What?" Grace mentally recoiled from the message. She typed a response and hit Send.

What are you talking about?

She waited, her frustration mounting as she watched the ellipses that confirmed he was typing a response.

Look around. See for yourself. I found evidence at his office.

This was insane. She sent another message.

Why were you at his office?

Reynolds found it...showed me. Get out of the house.

Grace didn't bother with a response. The man was playing some sort of game, and she was not going there. If she had to choose between trusting him or trusting Rob, she was going with Rob.

Still, she hesitated. There was the sports drink in the refrigerator. But he'd said he drank water mostly. So if it wasn't his, then whose was it?

She walked back to the refrigerator and opened the door. She moved the milk aside. It was still there— half a thirty-two-ounce bottle of red sports drink.

She shivered and slammed the door. There had to be a reasonable explanation.

But Gibbons's words had dug in their claws. She opened drawer after drawer…cabinet door after cabinet door. Found nothing out of the ordinary. No hidden files or surveillance photos of the inn or of her and Liam. Nothing that made her suspicious as to why Rob would bring them here.

Then she went to the main room. Scanned the shelves, the side tables and their drawers. She checked the coat closet…the powder room. Grace moved into the owner's suite then. She rifled through the drawers. Nothing. The same in the closet. Under the bed.

She was losing her mind. Gibbons had done this on purpose to make her doubt Rob. That would give Gibbons control.

She stamped out of the room.

Did Rob have an office here? He hadn't mentioned one.

She rounded the staircase and followed the narrow hall between it and the front exterior wall of the cabin. Sure enough, at the end of that little hall was a small room with a desk and chair. A laptop sat on the desk. A bulletin board adorned one wall. There were a couple of photos of him and his deputies, but little else. She chewed her lip. The top of the desk was clear save the laptop. It wouldn't hurt to have a quick look in the drawers.

As she took a deep breath, she moved around the desk and sat down behind it. Rolling back in the chair, she started with the middle drawer. She pulled it open, expecting to see pens and pencils and other miscellaneous office supplies.

Instead, she found newspaper clippings.

Her heart stumbled. Her fingers trembled as she picked through the array of clipped articles and the printed images of *her*...of Adam.

She wanted to believe these were gathered after the trouble started at the inn, but that was impossible. The clippings were from articles published in newspapers right after Adam's arrest. Dozens of them from the months immediately after that. Her trembling hands pushed them aside, only to find recent photos of her and Liam around town.

Why would he have all this?

Then her fingers touched something cold. She pushed the printed images and clippings aside and her gaze homed in on a chain. Silver. Rusty. No, not rusty—crusted with dried blood. On that chain was a locket. As if they had a mind of their own, her fingers plucked it up and opened the locket.

The small cut-to-size photo of her stared back at her.

The locket that had gone missing after she'd hidden it under the sink at the inn.

"Oh my God."

The sound of the kitchen door slamming and Rob's voice as he answered whatever question Liam had asked had her dropping the locket and easing the drawer closed. She hurried out of the room and down that narrow hall.

Her heart pounded so hard she couldn't catch a breath.

Maybe Gibbons was right. She had to get out of here until she knew for sure it was safe.

No. That couldn't be right. She knew Rob...

She came to a dead stop before reaching the kitchen. For well over a year she had thought she knew Adam. And look how that turned out. Didn't matter either way. She couldn't take the risk. For now, she could not allow Rob to see that she was upset. She had to be calm. Had to act as if nothing had happened. And then she had to get out of here...somehow.

It would be dark soon, and though she had paid attention to the landscape as they'd driven here, she wasn't sure she could find her way out on foot.

If she could get her hands on his SUV fob...

The voices were coming nearer. Her sweet little boy's baby voice and Rob's deeper one.

Her cell chimed. She jumped and checked the screen.

I'm coming. I'll bring help.

Gibbons was coming. Okay. They could straighten this out when he arrived. If Rob— She halted that thought. It just wasn't possible. Gibbons had to be wrong.

Finding those newspaper clippings and photos was one thing...but the locket. Had he found it and hidden it to protect her?

Or was he the one who'd planted the knife under the sink at the inn?

No. That couldn't be right.

Stop. She had to stop. All she had to do was stay calm and get through this. There would be logical explanations. There had to be.

She shoved the phone into her back pocket and hurried to the other short hall that led to the powder room and owner's suite. She did an about-face and started forward as if she'd only just come from the bedroom.

"Mommy! Mommy! I sit on horse!"

Liam's eyes were big, and his little body was literally vibrating with excitement.

Rob wore a big grin as if putting Liam on the horse had been almost as exciting for him. "I'm going to have to take him riding tomorrow. He loves the horses." His grin fell. "You okay?"

He searched her face, no doubt noting her emotional state as if the fear and desperation were written across her skin.

"I'm good." She shrugged. "I made the mistake of checking the news feed." She shook her head. "I shouldn't have."

"The media can get ugly." He made a sad face. "But it will pass."

How could he be so kind and just down the hall have all those things hidden in his desk?

"I should get Liam cleaned up for dinner. It's ready." She picked up her son, thankful he had on his shoes and coat. She could sneak out the kitchen door and hide until Gibbons was here and they had all this sorted out.

Guilt piled on her shoulders for thinking badly of Rob. He had been so kind to her and to Liam. But she could not risk Liam's safety for anyone—no matter how much she wanted to believe in Rob.

Rob's expression shifted to one of concern as he gazed past her at something outside. "There's a vehicle coming. You and Liam go in the kitchen. Stay out of sight until I see who this is." He shook his head. "Reynolds would have warned me if he'd sent anyone out here. Whoever this is, they shouldn't be here."

"Be careful." Her pulse was hammering now. What if this was a trap and Gibbons intended to hurt Rob? But why? It made no sense. Had this case pushed him over the edge?

Rob moved closer to the window. "Whoever it is has stopped on the other side of those trees. Out of eyesight." He bent down and removed a small handgun from around his ankle. He turned to Grace and handed it to her. "Go out the back door and into the barn. Hide in the darkest corner you can find. If anyone comes out there besides me, shoot first and ask questions later."

"Rob, I—"

"Go," he insisted as he headed for the door.

"Mommy?"

Liam's voice was full of uncertainty. Grace gripped the gun, lowered it to her side. "It's okay. We're going to play hide-and-seek. Rob will look for us, but first we have to hide."

Maintaining her balance with Liam in her arms, she shoved first one foot and then the other into her boots. She didn't bother to track down her coat. She rushed to the back door and slipped out.

Her cell chimed. She bit back a swear word, tucked the handgun into the waistband beneath her sweater and reached for her cell. Another text message from Gibbons.

Come to the woodshed.

Rob had said go to the barn. He'd given her a gun. Why would he do that if he was working against her?

"Mommy," Liam said. "We gots to hide."

She would check the woodshed, and then she was going to the barn. She hurried along the end of the cabin and surveyed the treed area between the end of the house and the barn. She could get to the barn without being seen from the front of the house. Then she'd have to slip around the back of the barn and through the corral to get to the woodshed without anyone out front seeing her.

She could do that.

Grace held Liam pressed close to her chest. She moved as quickly as she dared without risking a fall carrying him. She'd expected to hear Rob talking to someone by now. The good news was she hadn't heard any gunshots or other sounds of trouble.

She moved through the dark barn. The sun would be setting soon. She slipped out the back and through the corral. The horses at the water trough raised their heads and stared at her.

"Horsie, horsie," Liam said softly, his little voice muffled by her hair.

She held him tighter, tears burning her eyes. Her instincts were screaming at her. Something was wrong. *This* was wrong.

Finally she reached the woodshed. She paused to catch her breath, then reached for the door. The wood crossbar that secured it closed had already been removed, so all she had to do was pull it open.

The fading light filled the space beyond the door. Grace froze.

Detective Lance Gibbons lay on the floor. Blood soiled his shirtfront. He'd been stabbed over and over...just like Adam...just like Pierce.

"Grace!"

Rob shouted her name from the direction of the house.

He was looking for her.

She opened her mouth to answer but snapped it shut.

She couldn't be sure of what was happening. Her best option was to hide until she could figure out who was telling the truth.

She ran for the woods.

"Mommy, we hide!"

"Shh," she urged. "Yes, but he'll find us if he hears us," she whispered.

It was dark in the woods. Grace slowed. She couldn't see well enough to move fast.

A gunshot, then another rang out. She stumbled, almost fell. She darted behind the nearest tree and hovered there. She made soft shushing sounds to keep Liam quiet.

"We hidin'?" he whispered as best as an almost three-year-old could.

"Yes," she whispered back.

Gibbons was dead. The realization slammed into her all over again. Had Rob been shooting at someone? Or had someone been shooting at him?

Fear twisted inside her. She couldn't just hover here. She needed to get to a better hiding place or to find help.

Like that was going to happen. She was in the middle of nowhere.

She should call for help.

She pulled out her phone and tapped the necessary digits. But the call failed. She bit back a curse. No service. But she'd had service before she came into the woods. At least for text messages.

There was no time to figure it out. She had to hide.

ROB HUNKERED DOWN behind the unknown vehicle. It looked familiar but he wasn't sure. It was getting dark, so it was difficult to make out all the details, but someone in the tree line had shot at him.

He'd shouted for Grace, and then the shots had rung out.

She had his handgun, but she hadn't been the one to shoot at him. She'd gone in the direction of the barn. No way could she have gotten to the trees on the other side of the vehicle that had shown up unannounced.

This was someone who'd come for Grace and Liam. His first thought was Gibbons. The trouble Rob had with that theory was why the detective would turn like that. Was he so thoroughly convinced that Grace was guilty too?

Rob's cell vibrated, and he scanned the tree line again before pulling it from his pocket. Reynolds.

"Listen carefully," he whispered before Reynolds could speak, "I'm under fire here at the cabin. I need backup."

"Heading that way." The sounds of Reynolds running and then a vehicle door closing punctuated his words.

"I'm going to move toward the last known location of the shooter," Rob explained, "to make sure he hasn't started toward the barn where I told Grace to hide with Liam. I need you and anyone else you can get ahold of here as soon as possible."

"You need to know something," Reynolds said as he started the engine of his vehicle. "Cara Gunter disappeared today. Just vanished."

What the hell? Grace would be devastated if someone had gotten to Cara. "How did that happen?"

"You got me, but it gets worse," Reynolds went on. "When Cara didn't answer her cell, I went to her grandmother's looking for her. I thought maybe she'd gotten sick and Cara had to go to her. But old lady Gunter is dead, Rob. Has been for months. I'm guessing four or five, anyway. There are other remains with her. I can't be positive about anything beyond the fact that the remains are a younger female with blond hair. I don't know what to make of it, but Cara Gunter has been lying about taking care of her grandmother."

The realization of what that meant hit Rob like a sucker punch. "Gotta go," he said. "Get me some backup out here."

He'd have to analyze the news about Cara Gunter when he had this situation under control. He had to keep the shooter away from Grace and Liam.

Rob braced himself and made a dash into the open.

"HANG ON TO me tight, Liam," Grace said as she prepared to leave the cover of the trees. "We need to hide better."

"There you are."

"Cara!" Liam started wiggling, trying to escape his mother's firm hold.

Grace turned around. Cara was walking toward them. A rush of relief made Grace's knees weak.

Then she saw the gun in her friend's hand.

Grace tightened her hold on Liam, ignored his protests. "Cara, what's going on?"

Cara didn't stop until she was only a few feet away. "I have to get you and Liam out of here, Grace."

Heart pounding, Grace glanced at the weapon in her hand. "Why do you have a gun?"

Cara smiled. "Don't worry. I know how to use it." She shrugged. "For protection." Her attention zeroed in on the child in Grace's arms. "Liam, come to me."

It was all Grace could do to keep her son with her. "Be still," she ordered, fear funneling through her. "Cara, answer me. Why do you have a gun?"

It was almost completely dark now but not quite, and maybe even if it had been Grace would have spotted something different about Cara's eyes. They virtually glittered—the lightest, brightest shade of blue.

Like Adam's.

No, that was impossible. Cara had green eyes.

She laughed as if Grace had said the words out loud. "You see me now, don't you? I have the same eyes as him." She looked to Liam. "The same as his."

Grace stumbled back a step. Almost tripped over dead-for-winter underbrush. "I don't know what you're doing—"

"I do." She took another step toward Grace...toward Liam. "Do you have any idea how many fair-haired, pale-eyed women he had to go through before he found one who could give us what we wanted?"

Adam's victims—all with blond hair and pale eyes—flashed one after the other in Grace's mind. Then her own image stalled there.

"One couldn't get pregnant." She rolled her eyes. "She lied about that. Then DNA showed all these issues with the others. I suppose it had to do with the selection pool. I warned him about going so low-rent, but he was worried about taking someone who would be missed." She smiled. "And then he found you. Completely by accident and you were perfect.

And Liam is perfect." She stared at the boy Grace held tightly against her chest. "Come to me, Liam."

He tried to turn and see her. Tried to get loose from Grace's grip. "Don't listen to her, Liam. She's pretending so she can win the game. We still have to hide."

Cara's face twisted in a sneer as she stepped right up to Grace and jammed the gun under her chin. "Put him down. Now."

Grace slid her right hand between her and Liam. "You know you don't want to hurt him," she said, buying time.

"Of course not." Cara smiled. "He's mine. He was always going to be mine."

Fear and outrage rammed into Grace. She steadied herself. "Let me think," she pleaded.

Cara waved the gun in the air, but she remained toe-to-toe with Grace. "Put him down and we'll talk about how to handle this. I'm sure we can work something out."

"Okay. Okay. Just give me a moment." Grace glanced around as if uncertain, and then she hefted Liam higher with her left arm while snagging the handgun in her waistband with her right hand. She jammed the gun into Cara's body and pulled the trigger.

Nothing happened.

Cara stumbled back in surprise. Then she laughed. "Were you going to shoot me, Grace? You might remember to take it off safety next time."

Before Cara could stop laughing, Grace pivoted the thumb lever on the weapon and fired again. This time the bullet left the chamber and struck the other woman in the abdomen.

Cara lurched back a step.

Gun clutched in her hand, Grace wrapped both arms tightly around her son and turned to run. She bumped into someone.

Diane.

Grace froze. Her heart thumped against her sternum. Why was Diane here?

"You okay?" Diane asked, looking from Grace to Liam with concern.

Grace blinked.

Diane asked again, "Grace, are you okay? Is Liam okay?"

Tears flooded Grace's eyes. "Cara tried to—"

Liam started to whine.

"Shh, shh," Grace shushed him. "It's okay now."

"Really it's not," Diane said. She leveled a weapon at Grace. "Toss that little gun you're carrying and put my grandson down."

Grace felt the air leave her lungs. This could not be real. Maybe she truly had lost it and none of this was actually happening. Dear God, where was Rob?

The other woman's words reverberated in Grace's head. "Grandson?"

Diane smiled. "Adam was my son. Adele—Cara— is his twin sister. She wanted a baby so bad but she couldn't have one." Diane made a sad face. "So Adam promised her a baby." She motioned with her weapon. "Now toss the gun."

Grace allowed the handgun to fall to the ground.

"But," Cara announced as she joined the two of them, "Adam screwed it all up." One hand was pressed to her abdomen, blood seeping around her fingers. The other hand still held her weapon. "The bitch shot me." She glared at Diane. "Why haven't you killed her already?"

"Just shut up," Diane, or whatever her name was, growled before swinging her attention back to Grace. "Give Liam to me and we'll be done with this."

Grace understood that if she gave up Liam she was dead, and she could only imagine what would happen to her son then. Still, both these women had weapons, which meant running wasn't an option. Grace's heart twisted. Diane and Cara had been like family to her and she had never suspected a thing…because they were too good at hiding the truth and she had been desperate for a real family after losing her father.

An idea took shape. That was her only hope. *Family.*

"Why can't we share him?" Grace urged, her mind frantically grappling for a workable escape plan. "We've been like family all these months. We can make it work."

Where the hell was Rob?

Was he dead? Had one of them shot him? The memory of those gunshots echoing spiked terror in her veins. Her stomach dropped to her feet. *Please don't let him be dead or gravely injured.*

"She can't be serious," Cara—Adele said with disgust.

Diane threw her head back and laughed. When

she'd pulled herself together again, she demanded, "Why on earth would we do that?"

Liam's little body had started to shake. Grace had to do something fast.

"All right." Grace took a breath. "At least let me carry him back to the house. Give him time to calm down." His whining had turned to sobs now, the sound breaking her heart.

"Fine. Start walking," Diane ordered. "And remember we'll be right behind you. You make a mistake, and I'll put one in the back of your head."

Grace summoned her fleeting courage. The way she saw it, she had maybe five minutes to come up with a better plan since the chances of being rescued looked pretty slim at this point. Her gut clenched again at the idea of what had likely happened to Rob.

If he was dead... No, she couldn't think about that.

"I liked you, Gia," Diane said. "I knew you were the one when Adam finally found you, but then he had to go and do something stupid like take someone else. I thought he'd broken that nasty habit since you were pregnant with Liam and his promise to Adele was fulfilled. Guess I was wrong." -

"Ha," Adele snarled. "He liked that part. He was never going to stop. Once you get the taste for killing, there's no going back."

"Whatever his problems, you had no right to do what you did." Diane was the one snarling now. "He was *my* son."

"*He* is the reason," Adele fired back, "we're in this

mess. If he hadn't decided he wanted to keep Liam for himself, none of this would have happened."

Grace took her chance while they were distracted. She lurched forward, pretended to trip and fall to her knees. She set her son on his feet. "Run, Liam," she whispered in his ear before pushing him forward.

Diane snagged her by the hair and tried to pull her up. "Get up."

"Run!" Grace screamed, urging her son to go with every part of her being.

Liam rocketed forward.

"Liam!" Diane shouted.

"I'll get him," Adele grumbled.

As Adele took off and Diane watched her disappearing grandson, Grace twisted just enough to kick her in the knees with every ounce of strength she possessed.

Diane pitched sideways.

The gun flew from her hand.

Grace scrambled for it.

Diane hurled herself on top of Grace. Grabbed her by the hair again and slammed her head against the ground.

Pain reverberated through her skull. Grace rode it out. With all her strength, she bucked and clawed at the other woman's eyes. Diane jerked her upward once more and banged her head against the ground. Grace balled the fingers of her right hand and punched her in the throat. As Diane grabbed at her throat, Grace bucked her off. She clambered away, got to her feet.

Diane made a keening sound and scrambled after Grace.

"Don't move!"

At the sound of the deep voice, Grace froze, then whipped around.

Rob stood over Diane, the barrel of his weapon pressed against the back of her head.

She'd never been so happy to see anyone in her life. But her relief was short-lived. "Liam…" Grace surveyed the woods. Where was her baby? "Adele…" She turned back to Rob. "Cara is Adam's sister Adele. She's after Liam."

Rob cuffed Diane's hands behind her. He hitched his head toward the abandoned gun on the ground. "Watch her. I'll be back with Liam."

Grace grabbed the gun. "You watch her. I'm going after Liam."

She took off before he could argue. Her son would likely run to someplace he recognized…a place where he felt safe. He would reach the barn first… Maybe the horses were still there.

Grace ran through the darkness, straining to see the trees before she hit one. She wanted to scream for him but didn't dare. When she burst into the clearing by the barn, the exterior lights had flickered on, parting the darkness. Cara—Adele lay on the ground, her body writhing in pain. She'd dropped her weapon and was clutching at her belly with both hands. Blood had soaked into her blouse, rose up between her fingers.

The horses stood away from her, closer to the

barn as if they knew the woman on the ground was trouble.

Grace kicked the wounded woman's gun aside the way she'd seen cops do in movies.

"I need an ambulance," Adele moaned.

Grace ignored her. "Where is Liam? Liam!" She could call for him now that Adele was no longer a threat. "Liam! It's Mommy. Everything is okay now."

"Mommy!"

Her heart rushed into her throat as she looked frantically from side to side. Where was he?

The horses stepped apart and Liam stood between them. Had they been hiding him?

He rushed toward her.

Grace grabbed her son and held him tight.

Sirens wailed and lights flashed as two county SUVs bounced along the long driveway.

Grace dropped to her knees, unable to take another step.

Thank God.

Help was here.

And maybe…just maybe it was over.

Chapter Sixteen

Grace sat in the office belonging to Sheriff Tara Norwood. Grace had not slept all night. How could she? Liam had crashed around midnight. Rob had helped her lay him across the small sofa in the private waiting room.

Caffeine and adrenaline were all that kept her eyes open and her mind working, however sluggishly.

Adele—aka Cara Gunter—was at Erlanger hospital in guarded condition. The shot Grace had managed to pull off had lodged in a precarious spot next to an artery. Then all the running and attempting to grab Liam had caused it to move, creating a small tear. The evil woman was lucky to still be alive.

Diane Franks, the mother of Adam and Adele, was in custody. The FBI had arrived late last night and she had immediately gone for a deal. She was now singing like the lead vocalist in an out-of-control rock band. Apparently, there was a lot more to the

Locke family than anyone had known. Grace suspected even more would come out in time.

Diane claimed she had the twins when she was only sixteen, and she'd given them up for adoption—forced to do so by her parents. Later, she'd found them and taken them back after the adoptive parents had met with untimely deaths. She'd changed the twins' surname to Locke, her own as well. Then she'd married a man named Franks and gotten a job with the *LA Times*. By then the twins were adults and doing their own thing. But they always stayed together, oddly so. When they got into trouble, they ran to Mommy and she took care of them until the heat settled.

Adele had learned she couldn't have children, and Adam had decided to "make" one for her. After he was arrested, Adele had flipped out and was institutionalized. But her mother had promised that she would find her baby for her. It had taken Diane more than a year, but she'd finally found Grace. She'd made sure Liam grew attached to her, and then when her daughter was well enough to be released, they had found an identity for her to assume and inserted her into Grace's and Liam's lives by killing Kendall Walls and making it look like an accident.

Grace felt sick at the reality that Kendall had been murdered. On top of that, Diane had killed poor Mrs. Gunter and her daughter to give Adele a place in the community. Mrs. Gunter had been housebound and her daughter had moved away years ago, only visiting occasionally. So no one in the community realized that Adele wasn't her.

All the while, Adam had spent his time in custody deciding he wanted to keep his son for himself. He felt his mother and sister were ganging up on him. When he was suddenly released, he'd come to Lookout Mountain to change that situation.

Diane had lured Pierce to the inn to ensure there were plenty of suspects. Ultimately, she had hoped to see that Grace was charged with whatever had to be done—like murdering Pierce and Gibbons. Killing Adam wasn't part of Diane's plan. Adele had gone rogue with that one.

The FBI agent in charge had explained to Grace that she had nothing to worry about as far as Adam's followers. Any he had garnered eventually lost interest and moved on to newer and bigger headline grabbers. The others who wrote letters were just the typical jailhouse fangirls.

That part gave Grace some sense of relief. The rest, she thought as she stared at her sleeping child, was terrifying. She'd never wanted Liam to know about these people, but she wasn't sure how she could protect him from something this big. He had a grandmother and an aunt who were murderers.

Somehow she had to find a way to keep them from his life. Those people were responsible for her father's untimely death. They had murdered poor Val.

The sooner the two were extradited back to California, the happier Grace would be.

She had given her statement to Sheriff Norwood and the FBI, not holding anything back. Rob assured her she had nothing to worry about. She hadn't done anything wrong. She could take steps to legalize her name change and a good attorney could square things with the IRS related to her business operation the past few years.

Hopefully the community would see her side of all this and forgive her for all the secrets and lies. Sometimes a person just needed a place to hide and this little community had welcomed her with open arms. She didn't want to lose that.

The door opened slowly, and Rob peeked in before stepping into the room. She waved him in and he sat down in the chair next to hers. "I can take you home now."

Grace closed her eyes to hold back the tears that had been threatening for hours. When she could speak, she looked to Rob. "I honestly don't know where home is anymore. How can we go back to the inn with all those reminders of Cara and Diane? Will we ever feel safe there again?"

Rob took her hand in his. "You know you can trust me, right?"

Grace didn't doubt him. She'd shown him the clippings and the locket in his home office, and the sports drink in the refrigerator. They'd figured out that Cara/Adele had set him up as soon as she discovered that Grace and Liam were going there. The excuse that she needed to see about her grandmother was the perfect alibi for slipping out when no one was supposed to leave the inn. The open window in the bathroom at Rob's cabin should have clued Grace in.

"I trust you completely," she assured him.

"Liam saw nothing bad at the inn—other than the man in the snow. It makes sense that he would feel most at home there. How about we go back to the inn. I'll stay as a guest in one of the rooms for as long as you need me there."

Grace wanted badly to do that but… "Diane and Cara won't be there." This would be the hard part for Liam.

"He'll get used to them being gone, just as he did Kendall. Eventually you'll hire a new chef and a new assistant and things will settle down into a normal rhythm. I'll be there whenever you like."

As hard as she understood it would be, Rob was right. She and Liam needed to go home and work through the loss. "You're right. We should try."

"If it doesn't work out, there's always my apartment. I'll gladly put the two of you up there for a while."

Grace should never have doubted him. He was such a good man. Liam adored him and that meant a great deal to her.

She smiled, the first real one in days. "All right. If you're sure that's what *you* want. This is a big undertaking."

"I have never wanted anything more in my life." He hugged her. "Let's get you home."

Home… She hoped she could still call this place home. And she desperately hoped this man would always be a part of it.

Chapter Seventeen

The Lookout Inn
Mockingbird Lane
Lookout Mountain, Tennessee
Thursday, February 29, 5:00 p.m.

Grace shut down the computer and glanced around the lobby. She was finished for the day.

As she rounded the end of the counter, Liam came zooming through with his new toy airplane, making, of course, engine sounds. He and Rob had put the plane together two days ago and it had been his favorite toy since.

Grace wandered to the kitchen with the intention of starting dinner. There were no guests at the inn tonight, but she was fully booked for the weekend. The insanity of the Locke family murders hadn't hurt business one little bit. But the best part of the past few days was the reaction of the community. Everyone who lived on this part of the mountain had personally visited Grace and praised her bravery and fortitude. It was amazing. She blinked back tears even now. She cried every time she thought about how the community had come together in support of her and Liam. She wasn't sure how she had been lucky enough to pick this place, but she was certainly glad that she had.

Next week she intended to start interviewing for a new staff. The Wilborns were well and had returned to work. Their presence had been good for Liam—something constant. Both had gone above and beyond to keep Liam distracted from looking back. Karl planned to have him help with a small vegetable garden. Paula had come up with a plan to build a little chicken coop and enclosed run on the other side of the shed. Liam was thrilled at the idea.

And Rob. There were not enough ways to convey how much Grace appreciated all he had done. His presence evening after evening had made all the difference.

The sound of Liam's excited voice told her Rob was home—here. This wasn't his home and she had to keep reminding herself not to get too used to him being a part of their daily lives.

Rob pushed through the door to the kitchen wearing a big grin. "Don't cook," he said. "We're going out to celebrate."

Grace smiled. "What are we celebrating?"

He spread his arms wide. "Seven days free of the past."

Grace laughed. "You're right. We should celebrate." The idea of what this might mean tugged at her. They were doing great. This was true. "Does this mean you're ready to move back to your place?"

She held her breath. He'd spent every single hour off duty here since they came home from the sheriff's office that night…seven days ago.

His face turned serious as he stepped closer. "Does that mean you want me to move back to my place?"

She dared to breathe and without hesitation told him the absolute truth. "No. I like…you…here."

He moved closer still. Lowered his head so that his face was close enough to hers to make her heart pound like crazy. "I like being here."

She looked up at him…at his lips…into his eyes. "So you'll stay."

That grin spread across his face again. "I will. But don't worry. I'm not trying to rush things. We can take this as slow as you want."

Grace thought about the idea for a moment. Then she shook her head. "Forget the slow part. I'm ready to start the rest of my life." She draped her arms around his neck and pulled him closer still, kissed him firmly on the mouth.

That grin of his widened, the feel of it against her lips making her heart skip. "Works for me," he murmured.

He kissed her long and deep, and Grace knew with complete certainty that she was really home now.

* * * * *

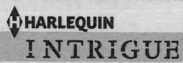
#2205 BIG SKY DECEPTION
Silver Stars of Montana • by BJ Daniels

Sheriff Brandt Parker knows that nothing short of her father's death could have lured Molly Lockhart to Montana. He's determined to protect the stubborn, independent woman but keeping his own feelings under control is an additional challenge as his investigation unfolds.

#2206 WHISPERING WINDS WIDOWS
Lookout Mountain Mysteries • by Debra Webb

Lucinda was angry when her husband left his job in the city to work with his father. Deidre never shared her husband's dream of moving to Nashville. And Harlowe wanted a baby that her husband couldn't give her. When their men vanished, the Whispering Winds Widows told the same story. Will the son of one of the disappeared and a writer from Chattanooga finally uncover the truth?

#2207 K-9 SHIELD
New Mexico Guard Dogs • by Nichole Severn

Jones Driscoll has spent half his life in war zones. This rescue mission feels different. Undercover journalist Maggie Caddel is tough—and yet she still rouses his instinct to protect. She might trust him to help her bring down the cartel that held her captive, but neither of them has any reason to let down their guards and trust the connection they share.

#2208 COLD MURDER IN KOLTON LAKE
The Lynleys of Law Enforcement • by R. Barri Flowers

Reviewing a cold case, FBI special agent Scott Lynley needs the last person to see the victim alive. Still haunted by her aunt's death, FBI victim specialist Abby Zhang is eager to help. Yet even two decades later, someone is putting Abby in the cross fire of the Kolton Lake killer. Scott's mission is to solve the case but Abby's quickly becoming his first—and only—priority.

#2209 THE RED RIVER SLAYER
Secure One • by Katie Mettner

When a fourth woman is found dead in a river, security expert Mack Holbock takes on the search for a cunning serial killer. A disabled vet, Mack is consumed by guilt that's left him with no room or desire for love. But while investigating and facing danger with Charlotte—a traumatized victim of sex trafficking—he must protect her and win her trust...without falling for her.

#2210 CRASH LANDING
by Janice Kay Johnson

After surviving a crash landing and the killers gunning for them, Rafe Salazar and EMS paramedic Gwen Allen are on the run together. Hunted across treacherous mountain wilderness, Gwen has no choice but to trust her wounded patient—a DEA agent on a dangerous undercover mission. Vowing to keep each other safe even as desire draws them closer, will they live to fight another day?

Get 3 FREE REWARDS!

We'll send you 2 FREE Books plus a FREE Mystery Gift.

FREE
Value Over
$20

Both the **Harlequin Intrigue®** and **Harlequin® Romantic Suspense** series feature compelling novels filled with heart-racing action-packed romance that will keep you on the edge of your seat.

YES! Please send me 2 FREE novels from the Harlequin Intrigue or Harlequin Romantic Suspense series and my FREE gift (gift is worth about $10 retail). After receiving them, if I don't wish to receive any more books, I can return the shipping statement marked "cancel." If I don't cancel, I will receive 6 brand-new Harlequin Intrigue Larger-Print books every month and be billed just $6.49 each in the U.S. or $6.99 each in Canada, a savings of at least 13% off the cover price, or 4 brand-new Harlequin Romantic Suspense books every month and be billed just $5.49 each in the U.S. or $6.24 each in Canada, a savings of at least 12% off the cover price. It's quite a bargain! Shipping and handling is just 50¢ per book in the U.S. and $1.25 per book in Canada.* I understand that accepting the 2 free books and gift places me under no obligation to buy anything. I can always return a shipment and cancel at any time by calling the number below. The free books and gift are mine to keep no matter what I decide.

Choose one: ☐ **Harlequin Intrigue Larger-Print**
(199/399 BPA GRMX)

☐ **Harlequin Romantic Suspense**
(240/340 BPA GRMX)

☐ **Or Try Both!**
(199/399 & 240/340 BPA GRQD)

Name (please print)

Address   Apt. #

City   State/Province   Zip/Postal Code

Email: Please check this box ☐ if you would like to receive newsletters and promotional emails from Harlequin Enterprises ULC and its affiliates. You can unsubscribe anytime.

Mail to the **Harlequin Reader Service:**
IN U.S.A.: P.O. Box 1341, Buffalo, NY 14240-8531
IN CANADA: P.O. Box 603, Fort Erie, Ontario L2A 5X3

Want to try 2 free books from another series! Call 1-800-873-8635 or visit www.ReaderService.com.

---

*Terms and prices subject to change without notice. Prices do not include sales taxes, which will be charged (if applicable) based on your state or country of residence. Canadian residents will be charged applicable taxes. Offer not valid in Quebec. This offer is limited to one order per household. Books received may not be as shown. Not valid for current subscribers to the Harlequin Intrigue or Harlequin Romantic Suspense series. All orders subject to approval. Credit or debit balances in a customer's account(s) may be offset by any other outstanding balance owed by or to the customer. Please allow 4 to 6 weeks for delivery. Offer available while quantities last.

Your Privacy—Your information is being collected by Harlequin Enterprises ULC, operating as Harlequin Reader Service. For a complete summary of the information we collect, how we use this information and to whom it is disclosed, please visit our privacy notice located at corporate.harlequin.com/privacy-notice. From time to time we may also exchange your personal information with reputable third parties. If you wish to opt out of this sharing of your personal information, please visit readerservice.com/consumerschoice or call 1-800-873-8635. **Notice to California Residents**—Under California law, you have specific rights to control and access your data. For more information on these rights and how to exercise them, visit corporate.harlequin.com/california-privacy.

HIHRS23